Merry Christmas, Kathy

Love, Mother + Daddy

1962

MYRTLE ALBERTINA'S SONG

Also by Lillian Pohlmann
MYRTLE ALBERTINA'S SECRET

Myrtle Albertina's Song

BY LILLIAN POHLMANN

ILLUSTRATED BY ERIK BLEGVAD

Coward-McCann, Inc.

New York

To Iris and Hal
with Love

Contents

MYRTLE ALBERTINA'S SONG

CHAPTER 1

Hare and Hound

MYRTLE ALBERTINA plodded happily along through the soft, white morning. As she went, stepping and sinking through the snow, she sang her thoughts. "Cozy white blanket over everything . . . everything, everything . . . over churches and houses and Indian campoody . . . over stores and gold mines and Chinese gardens . . . over fences and trees and birds' nests and squirrel holes . . ."

She was imagining the birds' nests and squirrel holes and mines but all the rest she'd seen from her own hillside as she waited for Tuley to come—everything in all directions humped under one great coverlet of snow.

Hugging herself to keep warm, she had tried to pick out places she knew, letting her thoughts burrow along under the whiteness like a quick little mole, up hill and down, in and out of friends' houses. They had followed the creek past Ah Sam's vegetable garden, found the courthouse and wiggled far under the pine trees where smoke was rising from the Indian campoody.

All the way to the woods with Tuley she'd remembered, planning how she would sing about it as soon as she was alone. "Cozy white blanket over ev . . . ery . . . thing in Eureka Hill this morn . . . ing." She tried to march as she sang and her footsteps marched behind her clean and deep across the sleeping meadow.

When she stopped to listen, the sound of Tuley's voice came to her clearly through the still, cold air. "Thirty-four, thirty-five, thirty-six . . ."

"He isn't even fifty yet," she whispered and went on, singing, panting out the words to make little white clouds of her breath.

"Sparkles . . . sparkles . . . everywhere . . . sparkles on the rocks, on the bushes, inside of me . . ." Grinning, she stopped to think. Yes, that was true. She *always* felt sparkly when she played with Tuley. And this playing Hare and Hound on a winter morning was . . .

12

"Forty-eight, forty-nine . . ."

"Oh, my goodness," she cried, "I'd better hurry." She stumbled on, stepping, sinking and planning as she went.

Here, of course, where the snow was deep, Tuley couldn't help seeing her footprints, but in the woods . . . where it had melted under the trees . . . She laughed. "I bet I can fool him this time. I bet . . . I bet."

"Fifty-two, fifty-three, fifty-four." He was counting slowly as he'd promised to do. She knew just how he looked, crouched beside her dog Major, back in the clearing, all set to follow her as soon as he reached one hundred. He'd be huddled, his collar turned up to his ears, his knitted cap pulled down to his black eyebrows and his breath steaming.

She stopped to puff warm breath into mittened hands over her tingling face, but only for a moment. As soon as Tuley's count reached seventy she made a muff of her coat sleeves and dashed for the woods.

For a while, shivering with excitement, she ran close to the tree trunks where her footprints wouldn't show. Then, laughing at the thought of how Tuley would wonder and wonder, she jumped wide and walked backwards. This made her tracks, which were *going* ones, look as though they were *coming*.

The woods were quiet except for the whispering water of the creek and the plop of the snow as it slipped from the trees. Thick pines and firs and cedars grew crowded together, closing out the light. Already it seemed more like afternoon than morning. Even the snowy caps on the rocks in the creek were bluish and shadowed.

Suddenly the sound of Tuley's voice seemed *very* far away. Almost like a tiny echo that wasn't saying *anything*. Almost as though there were no Tuley—like the time when she hadn't even known him.

That time seemed long ago. October, November, December, January . . . she counted on her fingers. Only four months since she'd met him in the woods. The weather had been snowing golden leaves that day. She smiled as she walked rapidly in and out between the trees, remembering.

Tuley and his father had been going to the Red Dog Mine and she had been coming from it. She and Major had taken Papa's lunch to him and Tuley and his father were going to take mining pictures to make into postal cards. Uncle Harvey had been carrying his long-legged, cloth-covered camera on his back and Major had rushed at him, growling. She couldn't blame him. Uncle Harvey, because he was dressed differently from most of the men in Eureka Hill, had looked strange to her, too, at first.

That had been before some stolen gold, or "highgrade" as the miners call it, from the Red Dog, had been found at Uncle Harvey's camp. Before Uncle Harvey's arrest. She and Aunt Eva had known all the time that there must be some terrible mistake. The wonderful part was when the sheriff knew it too—after Myrtle Albertina had shown him some gold she'd found accidentally, near the real thief's cabin.

The sheriff had told the whole town about the mistake, but some people hadn't listened. After Uncle Harvey married her own Aunt Eva, and opened a photograph gallery in the town, some still called him "the highgrader." At least that's what Skinny Hooper had told her.

That Skinny! He was as different from Tuley as anyone could imagine. Yet he was Tuley's friend. We . . . ll, she was Tuley's cousin *and* his friend. His *best* friend, she hoped, because he was certainly hers. She danced a glad hop-and-skip dance and stopped again to listen. There was no counting voice at all.

That means they've started after me, she thought, and raced ahead as fast as she could go. She climbed the long slope of Prospector's Hill and dipped down, slipping and sliding. She flew along the creek, trying to find a narrow place at which to jump . . . and stopped still. Instead of the familiar tracks she'd been notic-ing—the tiny fanned tracks of birds, the small paw-pad ones of rabbits, or the heart-shaped ones of deer—there, fresh in the snow, were dif-ferent tracks. They were shaped like a cat's and as big as her hand—mountain lion tracks.

Scary feelings mixed with her excitement and her heart beat a great thumpety-thump like the stamp mill at the mine. The paw-prints showed clearly as far as she could see, following the creek. She held her breath, looked all around and listened. All she could hear was the running whisper of the brook. Slowly she went on, one step and another and another, trying to think of Tuley's surprise when he found her footprints

side by side with a lion's. Maybe he'd suppose
. . . What would he suppose? She shivered and
giggled at the same time and went on even
more slowly.

When the sound of Major's barking seemed
also to fade away she stopped and tried to decide what to do. She hadn't meant for them to
really lose her trail. She jumped at the thud of
a pine cone on the snow, then whirled, pressing
her hand to her mouth as she heard a soft tread
behind her.

"Oh! " she gasped. "Oh, goodness, Young Joe!
You scared me."

When there was no answer, she smiled. "I'm
surely glad you're you. Because you could have
been a lion."

The boy, unlike Tuley, didn't smile back. He
stood tall and his square Indian face under
longish black hair, looked angry. He shrugged.
"Girl . . . crazy."

"No, I'm not," she faltered. "You know me,
Young Joe. I'm Myrtle Albertina Martin."

He pointed scornfully to the lion tracks.
"When you find lion, what you do?"

"Papa's your father's friend."

"Big Joe my father," the boy said.

17

"I know. Papa took Tuley and me to see you.
At your campoody. Remember?"

"Sure." He went right on glaring at her.
"Mountain lion maybe hungry in winter, huh?"

18

"I wanted to surprise Tuley."

"Maybe surprise lion instead. Not good." He moved around her and pointed. "Go."

"We're playing Hare and Hound. Don't

worry, I can hear Major barking now so I'll be all right."

"Go," he said.

"Well, all right." She turned and he followed silently behind her.

"Myr . . . tle Alber . . . tina." Tuley's call rang through the woods as Major's barking sounded suddenly, high and wild and near.

In a moment he bore down upon them, lifted his nose to catch the lion's scent and would have gone dashing by. Young Joe sprang, caught his collar and held him.

"Dog crazy, too." He looked sternly at Myrtle Albertina. "Go after lion, big trouble for him."

"I know." She bent down and threw her arms around Major's neck. "Stay!" she ordered. He whined and his brown eyes pleaded with her so hard to let him go that she had to laugh. "No, Major! Lions aren't good for dogs. Down!" she squealed as he gave her chin a lick. He lay panting with his red tongue hanging.

"Myrtle Al . . . ber . . . tina, wait. Wait for me!"

"Here we are, Tuley. Did you lose my trail?"

Tuley hurried toward them along the trail between the trees. "Say," he cried breathlessly, "I saw lion tracks with yours and I—"

She grinned. "I made them that way on purpose."

"Well!" he said angrily and turned to Young Joe. "Hello."

"I tell her go back," Young Joe said.

"I was going slowly, Tuley, only a little way. But you didn't come and you didn't come so . . ."

Tuley grunted disgustedly and kicked up flurries of snow.

"Come, dog," Young Joe called and bounded ahead with Major after him.

The morning was quiet again then except for the squeaky crunch-crunch of Myrtle Albertina's and Tuley's footsteps taking them out of the woods.

"Tuley."

He looked straight ahead. She thought he must know she was smiling at him but he wouldn't look. He had never been like this before, walking along with a dark face and making the fun go out of the day.

"Tuley," she said at last, "if it hadn't been for

21

the lion this would have been our very best
Hare and Hound game, wouldn't it? Tuley,
what's the matter?"

He hit out at a bush, making the snow fly.
"I should think anybody'd know better than to
fool around with lions."

"I do."

"Well, with lion tracks then. What if he'd
waited? What if a friend like Young Joe or
somebody wasn't around to help you?"

"I was scared. I wasn't going much farther,
Tuley. Honest I wasn't." She could see that he
was having a hard time making the frown stay
on his face and right away she felt happy again
—happy and sparkly and silly. Like giggling and
running and singing, because he really was the
best friend in the whole world.

"Can't catch me!" She started to run, skidded
and slid sideways into a snowdrift.

Instantly Tuley was over her, dropping a big
blob of snow. She felt it like a million cold stars
against her face and slipping down her back.
"Tuley," she squealed, "don't."

Tuley's face tried not to smile. "Well, what?"
he demanded.

"What what?" She giggled.

22

"What if sometime when you're not careful a friend wouldn't be around to help you?"

"I bet you'd be around, always."

Tuley shook his head. "That's the trouble. I won't. I think we're going away."

She felt a pinprick of snow against her cheek. She saw Young Joe wave good-by and she waved back. She saw Major come running and heard the stamp mill at the mine thumpety-thumping as it crushed rock so that gold could be removed. She could even hear the ore cars creaking on their small faraway tracks and the near purr of a breeze in the pine trees. Yet everything seemed scary still.

She swung to look at him but he turned away. "Going where?" she whispered.

"Far."

"Like Sacramento?"

"No."

"Where then?"

He shook his head, grinning a little.

"Oh Tuley, you're teasing me."

"No, I'm not. We may be going to the city to live."

"San Francisco?"

"For a while. Until we make some money.

23

Then maybe we'll go back to Cornwall. Or travel. See some of the world."

"Oh."

"Anyway, I'll be too far away to help *you* very much."

She started to speak but her voice wouldn't come. She dropped down beside Major and hid her face in his fur.

"Father says this country is fine for pioneers or natives or men who like to work in the mines. But we're Cousin Jacks and—"

"You are not. Cousin Jacks are people who've just come from Cornwall, England, and you've been here since you were a baby. Besides," she added in a muffled voice, "Aunt Eva is a native."

"Listen, Myrtle Albertina." Tuley pulled at her coat to make her look up. "Father says he wants to see some of the world and to know all kinds of people. But you know the real reason he's thinking of going away, don't you?" He tugged at her braids. "Don't you, Myrtle Albertina? Hey, look at me! I bet you'd like to see some of the world yourself."

"This is some of the world." She jumped up and rubbed the tears from her eyes. "It's Eureka

Hill. It's Mother Lode and Sierra Nevada and California and the United States and I like it, like it, like it."

Tuley laughed. "You're so mad you're scaring old Major."

"When are you going?"

"When school's out, I guess. Mom-Eva wants to go on teaching school till then. Besides she and father want me to finish out the term here." He sighed. "This is the only time I've ever had a chance to be in the same school for a whole year."

"You don't want to go away, do you?"

Tuley shook his head and bent to rub Major's ears. "It's the best year I've ever had."

"I won't let you go, then. I won't. I won't. Aunt Eva's our very own and now you are too. You and Uncle Harvey. You're part of our family."

"I know. I—" The blast of mine whistles interrupted him and Major raised his muzzle and howled. "Hey, is it lunchtime, already? I promised to help Father with some picture work this afternoon. Come on, Myrtle Albertina. Let's run."

"I don't feel like it." She plodded after him,

25

watching crystals of snowflakes melt on her mitten and thinking. "Tuley, who's going to take pictures of people if Uncle Harvey goes away?"

Tuley stopped to wait for her, scooped up a handful of snow and made it into a snowball. "Father says he won't even be missed. Not with the little business he does. You know, this is going to be a real water soaker, this snowball is." He tossed it from hand to hand. "Father doesn't really want to go away. It's just that people still treat us like strangers. That's the only reason he was ever suspected and arrested in the first place. You know that. Want to bet I can't throw this right into that old shaft over there?"

"Some people—"

"Hey, did you see that? Sailed it right in." He ran through the clean snow to the edge of the shaft and looked down. "This is really a deep one. I wonder if the fellow who dug it struck any gold."

"Tuley."

"What?"

"I meant that. About not letting you go away."

"All right, but I don't want to talk about it any more." He started to run. "Here, Major."

She dashed after him and reaching, caught the belt of his coat. "I won't let you go," she cried.

Tuley laughed and tried to jerk away but she held tight. "Pretty good . . . grip for a . . . girl," he puffed, ". . . glad we're cousins."

"What good is being cousins if you're going away?"

He didn't answer but went on jerking, stumbling and sliding down the hill, trying to shake loose. Major pranced and barked in wild circles around them and Myrtle Albertina kept her grip on Tuley's coat with cold, hurting hands until he tripped and they fell into a gasping, laughing heap in the snow.

CHAPTER 2

Uncle Harvey Makes Up His Mind

For weeks after that winter morning in the woods it seemed to Myrtle Albertina that Tuley liked to talk about going away so that she would grab him and cry, "I won't let you go." Since she no longer believed he was going, it was fun for her too.

Mama had set her mind at rest about that on the same day Tuley had told her. "They do talk of going," Mama had said, "but Eva tells me nothing's really settled. Your father and I, of course, are urging them to stay. And I know they'd like to, in spite of wagging tongues."

"Does wagging tongues mean talking?"

Mama had hugged her and laughed. "It means loose talk, Chick."

"Why doesn't everybody know by now about Uncle Harvey? That he was put in jail by mistake? The sheriff said so and the paper said so too."

"That's right. But he *was* in jail. To those who don't think, or won't, that seems to be a crime in itself. If only the reasonable ones would talk as much as the others we'd have no trouble getting Uncle Harvey to stay."

Myrtle Albertina had promised Mama as she'd promised Tuley. "I'm never, never, never going to let him go."

She'd promised it so hard that Mama had burst out laughing. "Fine, Miss Martin. You arrange that and we'll all be pleased."

Myrtle Albertina almost forgot about it as the months passed and no one said any more. Short little February disappeared while the rain was melting the snow and the cold was honeycombing the moist red earth with ice crystals. March flew by while swift white clouds pulled their big shadows over the new green hills. In April she and Tuley found the first lucky shooting star of the spring standing stiff and red-blossomed in a yellow patch of violets.

Now, already, it was May. Aunt Eva was still

teaching and Uncle Harvey was still taking a
few pictures in the photograph gallery in front
of their rooms on Mill Street. Tuley still waited
for Myrtle Albertina each morning at the foot
of her hill so they could make plans as they
walked to school—plans for playing or exploring
or being with other friends.

It was May and the plum tree outside Myrtle
Albertina's bedroom window was like a sweet
white cloud tied to a tree trunk. That's what she
was thinking as she sat under it trying to see
through to the sky.

The grass felt thick and springy-cool under
her hands, and when she lay down with her face
against it she thought she could hear it pushing,
pushing softly to grow. Everything pushing to
grow, she thought dreamily. Me too. She was
growing up with her body so that hems had to
be lowered, but inside too, she felt growing. She
let out her breath slowly, feeling strange and
still to think of all the growing going on in the
world, in the whole wide wonderful world . . .
in San Francisco and Japan and Africa and Den-
mark and . . . Her mind jumped over the
double-page map in her geography book, thinking how wide it was. Yet a map, she decided,

couldn't show the world really . . . a world's
highness . . . and deepness and air . . . and
animals and people. Its fishes . . . and birds
and plum trees . . . and me . . .

32

She turned over and sat up humming, trying words. "The world is deep and high and wide . . . the world is . . . wonderful . . . Eureka Hill's a world . . . this is a world, because . . ." She leaned back against the tree trunk. Because it's deep . . . What's deep? Deep is for mines, thumpety-thump. She laughed and leaned forward, hugging herself. If she could think of a high and a wide in Eureka Hill she'd have a sort of song.

Wide? Wide is for people . . . room for all people . . . hello to all people . . . Now, high. How can I tell how the mountains are? She watched the blossom petals turning, slow-falling as she put words together, until suddenly she sat up straight with surprise. "I've got my own song," she whispered.

She tried singing it, at first shyly, then louder and surer, over and over again. "The world is deep and high and wide . . ."

"Myrtle Alber . . . tina," Mama called from an open window, "time to come in."

"Mama," she cried, running into the house, "I've got my . . ." She started to tell what she'd been doing, but Mama was wearing her good plaid dress and the necklace of golden nuggets

33

Papa had given her before Myrtle Albertina was born. "Oh, company for supper! It's Tuley, isn't it, Mama? And Aunt Eva and Uncle Harvey?"

"That's right." Mama reached for a dishcloth and took a pan of saffron buns from the oven. Their rich yellow-flower smell filled the kitchen and Myrtle Albertina bent over them, sniffing.

"They're much too hot to eat yet, Chick. Listen, was that the gate? Papa already?"

Myrtle Albertina ran to the door. "Hello, Papa."

Papa threw her a kiss, gave her his lunch pail and, bowing to Mama, swept off his hat and put it on her head. Then he washed his hands and face at the basin on the back porch before he came in.

"Fee, fie, fo fum, I smell good old saffron bun." He tried to hug Mama and Myrtle Albertina and reach for a saffron bun all at the same time.

Mama stood in his way, teasing, with her apron spread. "None for you, Ed. You'll spoil your supper." She pretended to slap his hand. "Ed Martin, did you hear what I said?"

Papa winked at Myrtle Albertina as he tossed

his bun back and forth in his hands to cool. "You're looking mighty dressed up, Mary," he said to Mama. "Company coming?"

"Yes," Myrtle Albertina cried, "and I bet you can't guess who."

"No, but I can hope for the best."

"Like Tuley?"

Papa pretended to scowl. "Well, I was thinking of Tuley's parents. But if we have to have Tuley too . . ." He reached for her braids and she ran from him laughing and squealing.

"Mama, isn't Papa silly? Mama, what's the matter?" Mama's blue eyes were suddenly bright with tears.

"Don't notice me, Chick. I'm the one who's being silly. It's nothing," she said, trying to smile, but more tears came.

"Mary, what is it?"

Mama put her head on Papa's shoulder. "Why is it when a man is arrested by mistake, some people . . ."

Papa held her close. "You know why it is, Mary. A few, and, thank goodness, very few, are so darned disgruntled with themselves they don't trust anybody. Remember that kid we

35

knew, Johnny Somebody-or-other, they put in jail over at Tennessee Slide for stealing a horse? Lucky Jones' horse it was, remember?"

"What about him, Papa?"

"Well, Chicken, Johnny spent the night in jail and the next morning the horse was found right where Lucky's kid had left him, tied to a tree behind the schoolhouse. The sheriff was very sorry and let Johnny go right away. Lucky was sorry too and apologized. But some folks kept looking sideways at Johnny as if he *was* a horse thief. Got so, he told me once, having people act like that made him feel like he was. So he up and left town." He stopped and lifted Mama's chin so she would look at him. "Is Harvey fixing to do the same?"

Mama turned away and went to the stove without answering. She bent over to look into the oven, stood up, lifted a stove lid, poked at the coals and put in a fresh stick of wood.

Myrtle Albertina, forgetting to eat her saffron bun, watched her. She was feeling even worse than when Tuley had first mentioned going away, as though she were going down, down in the dark as she'd done once in the cage at the mine with Papa and some other miners.

Uncle Harvey Makes Up His Mind

That time the feeling had lasted for only a moment before the dropping stopped. Almost before she'd had time to gasp, the cage had stopped at an underground tunnel and she'd seen lighted candles on the front of miners' caps moving about like blowing stars. Then Papa had led her carefully through the earthy darkness to see the wide vein of gold which ran though the rock where he'd been working.

Now her going-down feeling wouldn't stop happening. "Mama," she asked, "is Tuley—"

"I don't want you worrying. I guess when Uncle Harvey makes up his mind he'll tell you."

It was Tuley, though, who told. Sitting at the supper table with the usual gay talk and laughter missing, he burst out. "I'll sure miss hearing old Major bark, or the stamp mills stamping, or the bands of cattle mooing along through town. Remember, Myrtle Albertina, that day they ran wild and stampeded, when Father and I boosted you and Mom-Eva over the fence and—"

"Son! " Uncle Harvey shook his head gently. His kind round face, usually so ruddy and jolly above his black mustache, looked troubled. His eyes moved from Tuley's face to Aunt Eva's and they smiled at each other in a way that made Myrtle Albertina think of the day they were married, when Aunt Eva, pink with happiness, had told them, "Mr. Stevens and Tuley and I are a family now."

"Yes, Tuley," Aunt Eva said, "that's right. But we'll hear new sounds, boats whistling, horsecars ringing." She tried to laugh. "Mary, Ed, won't you say something? What are you thinking?"

"We're thinking you should give the folks around here more time to get acquainted with Harvey." Papa reached to slap Uncle Harvey on the back. "What's the big hurry, old man? You haven't been smoked out yet."

"What's that mean, Uncle Ed?"

All the smiling went out of Papa's face. "I was only trying to be funny, Tuley. About something I don't feel funny about at all."

"But what does it mean, smoking out?" Tuley demanded.

"Sometimes in the old days miners let a fellow miner know he wasn't wanted by tampering with his chimney so smoke would fill his cabin and drive him out. It was a dirty business that stopped mighty fast when law and order moved in." Papa rumpled Tuley's hair. "I was only teasing your dad, but I don't like his talk about leaving his friends."

"We often wonder whether we have any, except for you," Aunt Eva said.

"You put too much stock in the talk of cranks." Mama stuck a spoon through the brown crust of a steaming meat pie and passed it.

"Ah," Uncle Harvey said, "Mary's famous meat pie. What could be better?"

"Mrs. Andrews is a crank," Tuley muttered. "Always saying things against everybody."

"Everybody except Kit Carson," Myrtle Albertina said. "She thinks he's just fine and likes him very much."

"Who do you mean, Chick? Kit Carson?" Papa was frowning.

"He's her cat. He's got his own collar with a buckle of real Spanish silver. Sometimes Mrs. Andrews takes him walking on a leash."

"She's the one I told you about, Father. Skinny talks to her all the time. She told him the men in her family had to sweat for every cent they got out of the mines so no highgrading thief was going to get off easy if she—"

"Tuley, shhh!" Aunt Eva put a finger over her lips. "I think Skinny must like to tell stories, don't you?"

Tuley flushed and, taking the full plate Papa passed to him, started to eat.

"Myrtle Albertina," Mama said, "please pass the salt. Mrs. Andrews is only one person and besides she's always thought the whole world was against her."

"You're right, Mary." Uncle Harvey rubbed a piece of meat in his gravy. "And I don't expect everyone to like me, or to think I'm an honest man. The real trouble is that I'm not doing enough business to keep us going. And certainly I'm not going to stay here and let Eva support us." He took an old battered copybook from his pocket and handed it to Papa. "There's my appointment book. Look at it."

Papa took it and flipped the pages, his face serious.

"Four appointments in the last three weeks and that's the way it's been going. The little photography I've had a chance to do has pleased people. I've heard that much. So there must be some other reason why I'm not getting more business."

Papa handed the book back to Uncle Harvey. "Can't you stick it out a while longer?"

"We plan to wait till school's out. If a miracle happens and things change by then, well, fine. If not, we'll try our luck in San Francisco." Uncle Harvey put down his fork and grinned at Mama. "If I had a few nuggets like those in your necklace, Mary, I could afford to stay around for a while. But I never was much good at prospecting, was I, Son?"

"That's because gold's hard to find, isn't it, Uncle Ed?"

"Mighty hard, Tuley. Don't forget that Mary's necklace came from my one lucky strike. Of course anyone who has time and patience might find something. But prospecting's always been uncertain, even in the old days. That's why I work in a big mine. The mine owners furnish the equipment, decide where the shafts are to be sunk and the tunnels are to be blasted. They decide where we'll work. Sometimes I find gold for them and sometimes I don't. But I always get my day's pay. I know," he said, smiling at Mama, "it's never quite enough to make ends meet. But it's sure." He turned to Uncle Harvey. "How about coming to work at the Red Dog with me?"

"No thanks, Ed. I'd had enough of tin mines in Cornwall before I came here. I thought mining for gold might be different, but it isn't. To me, all mining means leaving clean air and sunlight to go underground. I'd rather not do that. Not as long as there's another job I can do well and enjoy, like taking pictures."

"I understand, Harvey," Papa said. "Each man has to decide his own way."

For a moment the movement of knives and forks was the only sound. Myrtle Albertina cut a tiny square of pie crust and wiggled it through the gravy, but instead of eating it she looked at Tuley.

"Oh, come now, folks," Uncle Harvey cried, "let's enjoy ourselves together while we can. And anyway, San Francisco isn't the end of the world."

CHAPTER 3

Plans

FOR SEVERAL DAYS Myrtle Albertina tried to
think of ways to keep Tuley from leaving. It
seemed silly to her now that she'd promised she
wouldn't let him go. He'd have to go, of course,
wherever his father and Aunt Eva decided to
go.

If only . . . she would think to herself. If
only . . . And she would dream of something
wonderful happening, like hearing the sheriff
shout to everybody from the steps of the courthouse. "Folks of Eureka Hill! I urge you not to
let these fine people, Harvey, Eva and Tuley
Stevens, leave our town forever." Then she'd
have to smile, imagining Tuley's face if such a
thing should happen.

One morning she had a new dream. It started
with pretending, but the more she thought

about it the better it seemed. She dressed, lacing and tying her shoes impatiently so she could hurry downstairs in time to eat with Papa.

After breakfast, when he was ready to leave for the mine, she said she would walk a little way with him.

"Good," Papa said. "Ready to go?"

Mama kissed them both and outside Major met them, dancing and leaping. "He must think he's a young puppy again," Papa laughed.

Myrtle Albertina laughed too but she was thinking of something else. "Papa, where can I find some gold?"

"If I knew, I'd go get it."

"Well, you told Tuley if someone had the time or patience to look . . ."

Papa nodded.

"I have patience, Papa. And sometimes I have time."

"Forget it, Chick. This country's been worked over by prospectors for more than thirty years."

"I want to find gold for Uncle Harvey. So Tuley won't have to go away."

Papa slowed his long steps so that she could keep up with him. "When you really care for

44

your friends, Chick, you let them do as they think best."

"But Uncle Harvey did say if he had some nuggets like Mama's . . . Oh, Papa, I know he was fooling but if he really had some, he might stay."

Papa shook his head. "You can look if it'll make you feel any better," he said, "as long as you understand that you can't keep them here that way. They've pretty well made up their minds what they're going to do."

When they reached the bridge at the bottom of the hill he helped her to stand on the handrail, bracing her as they watched the bright water slide by under the willows and alders.

"May I dig then, Papa?"

"Dig away. Just as long as you're careful to stay away from old tunnels and shafts. Never go near those. You can start your digging at our old Frog Pond claim if you want to, but I think we worked all the gold out before you were born. Say, I have to get to work." He helped her down and gave her a pat. "Good-by, Miss Gold-Bug."

She waved until he was out of sight then

called Major and walked slowly back up the hill, planning. Planning, she walked around the house and up the back steps to the well. Mama must just have drawn some water because the heavy wooden bucket was shining with wetness. Myrtle Albertina drank, dipped some for Major and watched as he gulped it noisily.

"Mama," she called, "is it time to start for school?"

"Not for a while." Mama stepped busily out of the kitchen to the porch. "You and Major stay out here for a bit till the kitchen floor dries. I've just mopped and I don't want any tracks." She wrung a cloth out of a pan of water, twisting it hard.

"Mama, the Frog Pond's out by Lupita Martinez' place, isn't it?"

"Yes, in the gulch this side of there. Back of the Town Talk Road and a good long walk from here."

"Lupita walks it every day."

"Yes, I guess she does."

"I have to go there."

"My goodness, why?"

"For gold." Myrtle Albertina sat down on the porch steps in the sunshine. She untied her

46

shoelaces, pulled them tighter and tied them again. "If I can't find any . . . then Uncle Harvey . . . Tuley . . ." Suddenly she couldn't say any more.

Mama threw the scrub water out over the yard at the far side of the porch before she sat down beside Myrtle Albertina. "Gold's not to be had just for the digging, Pet. You heard Papa and Uncle Harvey say that. Tuley will be your friend wherever he is, you know that. Besides after he's gone, you'll find you can enjoy other friends very much too, like Annette and Lupita and Ruby Pearl and—"

"I do enjoy my other friends," Myrtle Albertina sobbed, "but Tuley's the best."

"I know." Mama held her close. "But you wouldn't want Uncle Harvey to stay here and be unhappy. Any man worth his salt has to support his own family, Chick. Now you just remember what Uncle Harvey said. San Francisco isn't the end of the world."

"It's far though."

"A hundred seventy miles or so. That's all."

"I want Tuley to live *here*. So we can play together."

Mama stood up and breaking a sprig of blos-

47

soms from the plum tree, rubbed it across Myrtle Albertina's nose. "Listen, young lady, you're worrying about things you can't do much about. Instead of thinking of something you can do."

"What, Mama?"

"Oh, something nice for Tuley before he goes."

"Like a party?"

"If you think that's what he'd like."

"A big one?"

Mama nodded.

"Can we afford it, Mama? You told Papa we'd have to scrimp to make the payment on our house."

"Oh my." Mama laughed and clapped her hands together. "Well, Miss Big-Ears, we have scrimped and now, for your information, it seems we can manage the payment. Let's see now, school's out on the seventh of June. So let's set the tenth for a party."

Myrtle Albertina wiped her arm across her eyes and felt herself smiling. "Would Aunt Eva and Uncle Harvey and Papa and other grown-ups come too? "

"Whoever you want."

48

Myrtle Albertina jumped to her feet and ran to hug Mama. "I think I want *everybody*."

"All right then. The tenth's almost a month away but I'd like you to take a note to Madame La Rue today. After school. Many ladies in this town have Madame La Rue help them with parties. She's French and a wonderful cook."

"Oh, that's a fine idea, Mama." Myrtle Albertina started to sing. "All our friends, all our friends, all our friends to a party."

"Well, that's better," Mama exclaimed as she carefully tiptoed across the still-damp floor to stir the stew on the stove. "In this house singing works better than tears."

Toot . . . Toot . . . Toot . . . Toot. The mine whistles blasted four great blasts into the morning. Myrtle Albertina looked at Mama and smiled. "Time for Papa to go underground and start to work."

"Time also for a certain young lady to start to school. Get your books together while I write a note to Madame La Rue."

That note tucked away in Myrtle Albertina's pocket helped her to keep a pleased feeling all day. When Tuley promised to go with her to deliver it she had to smile to think how surprised he would be if he knew what it was all about.

Madame La Rue's house was high on a hill so they could look up and see it long before they reached it. It was big and white and had a cupola. Wide steps led up to the front porch and in front, on a narrow strip of lawn, was a neat sign, BOARD AND ROOMS. The letters B and R were huge and painted with curlicues. The curlicues made Myrtle Albertina think of Annette La Rue, who was very lively and always wore ribbons on her curly hair.

Sure enough, when Annette answered their knock, her brown eyes and her blue ribbons were dancing. "Oh hello, Myrtle Albertina. Hello, Tuley. Did you come to play with me?"

"I came with Myrtle Albertina," Tuley said, grinning.

"And I came to bring a note to your mother."

Annette made a little face and ran back down the hall. "*Maman, Maman,*" she called.

Myrtle Albertina and Tuley smiled at each other and waited.

"Isn't Annette pretty?" Myrtle Albertina whispered.

Tuley shrugged. "I can just see *her* tracking a lion."

"But Tuley—"

He dived and stood on his hands, turning cartwheels around her.

"Hurry, Tuley, stand up. Here they come."

Tuley landed on his feet and tried to look serious just as Madame La Rue came to the door.

She was a small woman with flashing dark eyes. "*Bonjour.* You wish to see me?"

"Come in," cried Annette, pressing through the doorway in front of her mother, "come right in."

"Annette!" Madame La Rue's voice was sharp. She shook her head at Annette and turned to Myrtle Albertina. "Now, children, what is it?"

Myrtle Albertina could feel that something was wrong. Puzzled, she searched Madame La Rue's face. Madame La Rue was looking at Tuley and she seemed puzzled too.

Tuley flushed. "It was Myrtle Albertina who wanted to see you, Madame La Rue."

"Very well. Come in, Myrtle Albertina. And you, Annette."

Annette pouted. "I want to stay out here with Tuley and play."

"Annette."

Annette tossed her head and her dark curls

52

shook but, just the same, she turned and walked in.

Myrtle Albertina's face burned as she stood, not knowing what to do. She looked at Tuley but he turned away from her and ran down the steps. "I'll wait for you here by the gate," he called.

"Poor boy," murmered Madame La Rue as she led Myrtle Albertina into the house.

Myrtle Albertina blinked fast and swallowed hard but the tears came anyway. They blurred the parlor with its tasseled drapes and golden frames, so different from hers at home. The tears ran down her cheeks and she shook them away angrily.

"Why did you call Tuley a poor boy?" she faltered.

"Because some people say his father's a high-grader, that's why," Annette whispered loudly.

Madame La Rue threw up her hands. "What a naughty girl you are today, Annette. How many times have I told you, do not talk back to your *maman.*"

"Please excuse me, Madame La Rue, but I am going now. I don't want Tuley to wait all alone."

"Wait, Myrtle Albertina, tell *Maman*," Annette urged. "Tell her about Tuley's father. Listen, *Maman*, Myrtle Albertina knows all about it. She was the one who told the sheriff about the real thief."

Myrtle Albertina edged toward the door, shaking her head.

"Why did you wish to see me, Myrtle Albertina?" Madame La Rue asked.

"Mama sent me to ask you about a party, but . . ."

"Well? What about a party? Oh come back, child. Come back and sit down. Annette, go cut three pieces of cake. Set them out on a tray but don't bring them till I call you."

Annette ran and Madame La Rue gently pushed Myrtle Albertina to a chair. "Would you like to tell me about Tuley and his father?" she asked.

"If you knew them you wouldn't think . . . you wouldn't . . ."

"That may be very true." Madame La Rue's eyes, so like Annette's, became soft as velvet.

"Didn't you read about it in the paper? What the sheriff said and everything?"

"If I did, I've heard so much since that I . . ."

"All right then." Myrtle Albertina sighed and ran her hands over the deep green plush of the chair. "This is the really true story."

As she talked, Madame La Rue sat with her hands folded in her lap listening in a way that made it easy for Myrtle Albertina to go on. She started with the day she'd arranged with Uncle Harvey to have her picture taken for Mama. "Only of course he wasn't my uncle then because he hadn't married Aunt Eva." She told the whole story of the stolen gold. ". . . And after he and Aunt Eva were married, we had a birthday party for Mama. All of us together. Then Aunt Eva, Uncle Harvey and Tuley went to live on Mill Street and Uncle Harvey started his photograph gallery."

Madame La Rue smiled. "So that is the end? "

Myrtle Albertina shook her head. "That's the good part. The bad part is that they're going away."

"But why, if—?" Madame La Rue stopped and, blushing, looked at the ceiling. "Is it that nobody takes trouble to stop untruth?"

"It's because he hasn't enough business. He takes very good pictures, too. The one I gave to

Mama was colored and she liked it very much. Wouldn't you like to have a colored picture of Annette?"

"Yes, I would like that." Madame La Rue jumped to her feet and went to the door. "Annette," she called and turned again to Myrtle Albertina. "So, I will arrange with your uncle and," she snapped her fingers, "we say *pooh* to false talk. Oh, here we are," she said as Annette came into the room carrying a tray on which were three pieces of cream cake on three blue plates.

"I think I should go now, Madame La Rue," Myrtle Albertina said, "Tuley—"

"Nonsense." Madame La Rue handed her a plate. "Stay where you are. You will not mind if I do not eat with you. I do not care for sweets in afternoon. Annette, you and Tuley eat your cake outside while we talk business. Careful," she called as Annette ran out, "do not drop something. Now, Myrtle Albertina, what is it about a party?"

Myrtle Albertina handed her Mama's note and watched her eyes snap as she read it. "Your *maman* calls me best cook in Mother Lode," she said, laughing so gaily that Myrtle Albertina laughed too. "*Certainement.* Tell your *maman* I shall arrange all. She did not say what is the date. Do you know?"

Myrtle Albertina swallowed the last bite of cake. "It's the tenth of June," she said, "after the end of school."

CHAPTER 4

Whistles

Tuley hadn't eaten Madame La Rue's cream cake.

"I didn't feel like eating," he told Myrtle Albertina as they started home. "I guess you know now what Father was talking about," he went on angrily, "and why he doesn't get enough business."

"Tuley, it's going to be better after this. Madame La Rue promised and—"

"Oh, promises!" Tuley said.

Myrtle Albertina started to tell him what had happened but she changed her mind. There was so much she still couldn't understand. Why, just because one person didn't know another person, should she believe . . . ? Why should . . . ? She wanted, suddenly, to be home talking things over with Mama. But first, more than

59

anything else, she wanted to make Tuley happy again.

"Want to see some special Indian dishes?" she asked.

"Where? Why special?"

"The biggest. In Indian Dish Rock. We can take the path around Sugar Loaf Hill. Come on."

"I've seen lots of Indian dishes," he said. "They're bowls in the solid rock."

"I know. The Indians wore them down grinding meal, deeper and deeper and smooth as anything. They'd put acorns in them and smash and grind and . . . Beat you," she called, starting to run.

"Oh no, you won't." He flew by her and, reaching the rock first, swiftly brushed pine needles away from the top of it with his hands. "Here's one."

"Here's another. And here's the biggest. Look, Tuley." They were both laughing as they threw pine needles in all directions.

"Here's the biggest," he yelled.

Then they stopped and didn't move at all. The mine whistles were blowing. *Toot . . . Toot . . . Toot . . . Toot . . . Toot.*

Whistles

"Hey, Myrtle Albertina, why are the mine whistles blowing now? It isn't quitting time yet."

For a moment she didn't answer. Fear was running through her as soft and shivery as little gray mice, for she knew why the whistles were blowing. Except for starting-to-work time, lunchtime and quitting time, they blew for only one reason.

"Something's wrong. Oh, come on, Tuley, hurry. Maybe it's Papa's mine. Maybe it's a cave-in."

She thought only of Papa as they ran. She thought of him standing on the bridge with her that morning. She thought of him underground and remembered how he'd explained to her about the big timbers that were braced over-head in the tunnels to keep rocks and dirt from falling on the miners. Sometimes one of these loosened or broke and caused a cave-in in which someone could be hurt.

As they ran around the hill and down the steep wooden steps that led to town, the whistles kept right on blowing. When they reached Main Street they saw a crowd of people standing in front of the Wells Fargo office. Others

were running down the middle of the street or hurrying along the high board walk. Some stood at windows and all had questions in their eyes.

Mr. Hartung, who owned the livery stable next door to Uncle Harvey's, was standing under the big poplar tree in front of the hotel, shading his eyes as he looked toward the courthouse.

"Cave-in, Mr. Hartung?" shouted Tuley.

"No telling, son," Mr. Hartung shouted back, shaking his head. "It's some kind of trouble, that's sure."

Mrs. Andrews leaned from an upper window in the hotel. "I hear it's a terrible cave-in," she called.

The sheriff, with Dr. Dunn on the seat beside him, drove his horse and buggy wildly out past the courthouse toward the hills.

"Headed for the Red Dog, looks like," Mr. Hartung said.

"They say Red Dog," yelled a man in the street to Mrs. Andrews in the window.

"There they go," shouted someone else. "Yep, it's the Red Dog all right."

"Let's go around the corner to our place," said Tuley, "and tell Mom-Eva."

Red Dog . . . Red Dog . . . Red Dog . . .
The words were happening in Myrtle Albertina's head but she couldn't say them. Her fear
wasn't just a small shivering any more. It was
big and shaking.

"Maybe Papa's home already," she said,
"laughing and talking to Mama, washing the
mine dirt from his hands and—Tuley, I want
to go home. I want to see Mama right away."

"All right. Look, there's Skinny Hooper. Hey
Skinny, where you going?"

"Hello, Tuley. Hello, Myrtie." He was out of
breath and his pale blue eyes were round with
excitement. "I'm going to the mine. My pop's
out there. Come on."

"Myrtle Albertina wants to go home first. Her
father works at the Red Dog, too." Tuley started
after Myrtle Albertina, who was running again.
"See you later, Skinny. Good luck."

They ran till their breath stuck in their
throats and their sides ached. They ran till a
horse and wagon drew up beside them. "Oh,
Mr. Cunningham," Myrtle Albertina gasped,
"are you going to our house? Will you give us
a ride?"

"Sure thing. Have to deliver your milk and

butter anyway. Hop up. And your friend there, too. All right, now. Giddap, Lady."

"Do you think there's big trouble at the mine, Mr. Cunningham?" Tuley asked.

"Trouble?" Mr. Cunningham snapped the reins. "Trouble, sure. But trouble isn't always big trouble, boy. You just remember that." He nudged Myrtle Albertina. "You hear me, young lady?"

"Yes sir." She felt better already. About a million little white clouds raced across the sky, a yellow bird sang from the bridge rail as they started up the hill and Mama, waiting with Major at the gate, waved to them.

But when they stopped, Myrtle Albertina's heart started to pound for she could see at once that Mama was deeply troubled. She helped Myrtle Albertina down. "I'm glad you've come, Chick. And you, too, Tuley. Mr. Cunningham, could you please do me a favor? I've had word from the Red Dog and I'd thank you to take me there."

"Glad to, Mrs. Martin."

"Mama, is Papa—"

"Now listen, Pet," Mama said, "there has been a cave-in. The tunnel where some of the men were working is closed. But I've been told that many men are working to open it again." She took Myrtle Albertina's face between her hands. "Remember, we don't know that any-one's hurt."

"Take us with you, Mama."

Mama pulled her white shawl around her shoulders and gently shook her head. "I've left meat pasties in the oven and I don't want them to burn. Take them out when they're golden brown. Tuley, will you please keep the fire go-ing till they're done? I'll be back soon, I'm sure." She patted his shoulder, kissed Myrtle Alber-tina and climbed up beside Mr. Cunningham.

Myrtle Albertina watched the wagon until it was out of sight. She watched Major chase it down the hill and, when no one called him to come back, saw him come back anyway.

"We'd better go inside, Myrtle Albertina," Tuley said, "so we can see about the pasties and the fire."

Without a word she turned and followed him. Even when there was so much worry already in her heart, she remembered that he was going away.

CHAPTER 5

Another Home

EUREKA HILL wasn't like Eureka Hill at all with neither Mama nor Papa in it. That was Myrtle Albertina's first lonely thought when she woke the next morning. Her next was that she couldn't yet feel belonging in this strange bed in the corner of Uncle Harvey's photograph gallery. But in this room where Uncle Harvey had to arrange backgrounds for his pictures of people at a moment's notice, everything seemed unbelonging.

Near the foot of her bed were two huge, make-believe ferns in brown pots, and against the wall was a fancy garden gate twined with paper flowers. There was a chair like a throne with her clothes hung on it, a stone pedestal held a pitcher of water and a washbasin and, right beside her bed, her shoes stood neatly in the middle of a big white bearskin rug. She had to smile a little when she saw them because they looked lonely too.

She lay very still listening to the sounds of jingling harness and stamping horses that came through the walls from the livery stable next door. Shining slices of sunlight squeezed through the wooden shutters and made her think of her windows at home, wide open to the light and a plum tree in bloom. But all she was really thinking about was Papa and Mama. Her loneliness for them was a hurt in her stomach and her wanting to know about Papa was the biggest feeling she had.

Papa had been hurt in the cave-in. His head had been cut and his leg broken. Even so, he'd thought he was a very lucky man. He'd told Mama that if some of the timbers hadn't held and if the men digging to reach him hadn't worked so fast and carefully, it might have been a different story.

Myrtle Albertina closed her eyes and thought of Mama as she'd talked about it all, the night before. Dr. Dunn had taken Papa to the hospital in Gold Town and had asked Mama to go there too, to help take care of him. While Mama packed, Myrtle Albertina stood near holding the lamp.

"Papa was very cheerful and I think by going to him, I can help keep him from worrying." Mama had stopped and rested her hands on the edge of the big straw suitcase. "You'll like staying with Tuley, won't you, Pet? It will be a fine chance to have a lot of fun with him before he goes away." Her hands were busy again, folding things and tucking them in. "Dear, I'm afraid we can't plan on the party now. We have no way of knowing when Papa will be well enough, and with expenses . . . Will you tell Madame La Rue?"

"Aunt Mary," came Tuley's voice. "Here comes the horse and buggy from the livery stable."

"Go tell Tuley I'm coming," Mama said and Myrtle Albertina did, almost running into him in the dusk.

"I'm going to stay at your house," she said.

"I know. I'm glad."

"You know something, Tuley? There's a star right over your shoulder."

Tuley laughed. "I'll get your mom's suitcase."

71

After he'd lugged it down the steps, Mama had clung to Myrtle Albertina, seeming to want to say more and not having much time. "Take the pasties to Aunt Eva. Be happy and don't worry about Papa. Just remember the doctor said he'll be all right. I'll send you a note soon."

Myrtle Albertina sat up, yawning and hugging her knees. "Don't worry" had been almost Mama's last words to her and here she was doing only that. I guess if Papa thinks he's lucky, you can think so too, she told herself, and she stretched her arms wide just as a horse whinnied next door.

Bounding out of bed, she ran to peek through the shutters. All she could see was one tree with new pointed leaves unfolding—the one the Chinese people called the tree of heaven—the high brick wall behind the stable and sunlight spilling everywhere. It was enough to make her feel good again. Like getting things done. Like giving Madame La Rue Mama's message about the party. But most important, like working on her plan to keep Tuley in Eureka Hill.

Quickly she dressed, washed her face and made the bed. As soon as she opened the door into the kitchen, Major rushed to meet her, leaping so joyously that dust specks rose from his fur and danced along the sunbeams in the room.

"Good morning," sang Aunt Eva. "It's a good thing it's Saturday, so you could sleep late. Aren't you starved? Look here, a big saffron cake. Skinny's mother brought it. Said she couldn't help thinking about us because her husband was working right beside your father and wasn't hurt at all. Except for a few scratches."

"I guess Skinny's glad about that. But Papa's going to be all right, too."

"That's right."

"Where's Tuley?"

"He had his breakfast an hour ago." Aunt Eva opened the small doors at the front of the stove and blew on the coals until bright points of flame rose from them. "Your Major dog seemed to sleep here very peacefully last night," she said as she stuck a fork into a slice of bread and held it close to the fire. "I hope you did."

"Yes, I did. That toast makes me feel hungry. But Aunt Eva, you didn't tell me about Tuley."

"The person I want to tell you about is your

73

Uncle Harvey." Aunt Eva looked pleased and excited. "Early this morning he started out to the Red Dog to ask the mine boss if he could work for your father. In his place, till he's well again. He hasn't come back and I'm sure that's just what he's doing."

"But Uncle Harvey hates underground."

"He does indeed." Aunt Eva's face was lighted. "Making up his mind to do this for Ed was probably one of the hardest decisions he's had to make for a while. Oh Honey, someday when you're old enough to think of marrying, I hope you'll find someone as good as your Uncle Harvey. Or your own Papa. When I think how lucky I am to be Mrs. Harvey Stevens, I could sing. Even when it means leaving this town I love to live somewhere else."

"Won't Uncle Harvey make enough money at the mine now to stay?"

"Heavens, no. You know how he feels about making our living that way. No, he's only working at the mine so Ed can get his wages as usual."

"That's wonderful."

"I think so too. Here's your breakfast." Aunt Eva kissed the top of Myrtle Albertina's head and gave her two buttered slices of toast, a bowl of applesauce and a glass of milk.

"I want to know where Tuley is."

Aunt Eva laughed. "So, he's the only really important one in this family, is he? Well, he's working, doing some darkroom work for his father."

"Can he do that alone?"

"I guess so. He's been Harvey's right-hand man for a long time. What would you like to do, today?"

"I'd like to see Mama and Papa."

"I'm afraid you won't be able to do that for a few weeks. But Uncle Harvey has promised to drive us to Gold Town while your folks are there."

"Tuley, too?"

Aunt Eva nodded and dropped a bar of yellow soap into the dishpan.

Myrtle Albertina ate her last bite of applesauce and handed her dish to Aunt Eva. "Is Tuley going to work all day?"

"Most of it. He and Harvey had planned to have a big batch of postal cards ready to sell to the Miner's Union before we go."

"Then I think I'll be busy all day, too."

After Myrtle Albertina had helped with the dishes she took the pasty and apple which Aunt Eva had put in a paper bag for her and started out.

If it hadn't been for thinking about Papa, it would have been a truly dancing day. Dancing sunlight, breezes, leaves and grass. Even her feet couldn't keep from dancing as she walked because she felt so different from herself. She felt like some interesting girl who lived downtown in a photograph gallery instead of Myrtle Albertina Martin, who lived in a small house on a hillside. She was someone who lived next door, not to fields and a pine forest, but to a livery stable with horses. She walked slowly, watching her reflection in the windows of the dry-goods store and the Shanghai Restaurant, smiling a little. She still looked like Myrtle Albertina.

She paused at the door of the Columbia Hotel to say good morning to Mrs. Andrews, who was just coming out, leading her gray cat on a leash.

"Good morning, Myrtle Albertina. Please, hold your dog."

"Major wouldn't hurt Kit Carson, would you,

Major?" Major looked shy and waited, panting.

"Good dog. Very good dog," Myrtle Albertina said, then reached to pet Kit's shining fur.

"How's your poor father, Myrtle Albertina?"

77

"Dr. Dunn says he's going to be fine."

"Well, I hope so." Mrs. Andrews clicked her tongue and sighed. "You can never be sure, though." She shook her head. "Besides, there's hospital bills and the time lost from work."

"Uncle Harvey's taking care of that for us. He hates to work underground. But he's doing it because he likes Papa so much."

"Well. You don't say! That is a surprise." Mrs. Andrews lifted Kit Carson, wrapped his leash around her wrist and rubbed her cheek against him. "I'd heard your aunt's husband was leaving town."

A quick thought came to Myrtle Albertina, that Mrs. Andrews looked like a busy bird with a bobbing head and quick darting eyes.

"If they let him work at the Red Dog after what happened last fall, I'll be much surprised." Mrs. Andrews seemed to be talking to herself. "And if they do, they—"

"You know Uncle Harvey didn't have anything to do with that, Mrs. Andrews," Myrtle Albertina burst out.

Mrs. Andrews wasn't listening. She was calling to a woman in front of Van Metre's drugstore and in a moment was hurrying across the

78

street to join her. "Be a good girl, Myrtle Albertina, while your folks are away," she called back.

Myrtle Albertina swallowed angrily and twisted her fingers around Major's collar. "You be a good girl too, Mrs. Andrews," she muttered, "instead of saying bad things and never listening at all."

She kicked along the wooden sidewalk and past the Wells Fargo without once stopping as she usually did to look at the old posters about stagecoach robbers. Major whined and licked her hand. She knew he was trying to make her speak to him but she couldn't. Her tears wouldn't stay back, and besides she was lonelier for Mama and Papa than she'd ever been in her life before.

She stumbled along Poplar Lane, but when she faced into the sunshine to climb the steps to Madame La Rue's, she stopped. She blinked, blinked again, waited a minute, climbed five steps, then sat down and threw her arms around Major.

"You know what the sun's doing, Major?" she whispered. "It's turning my tears to rainbows in my eyes."

CHAPTER 6

Digging and Tamales

A H, YOU THINK I have forget the promise," exclaimed Madame La Rue as soon as she saw Myrtle Albertina at the door. "You think I forget to ask uncle to photograph Annette. But I have not."

She talked fast with her eyes flashing until she remembered Papa and stopped right in the middle of a sentence. "Your papa, Myrtle Albertina? Tell me first of him. He will be fine, yes?"

Myrtle Albertina told her about Papa and Mama, and gave her Mama's message about not having the party. She also explained that Uncle Harvey probably wouldn't be able to take any pictures for a while because of what he was doing for Papa.

"Ah, that is most remarkable," Madame La Rue said. "That shows most clear that what you have told me is true. So, with the Uncle Harvey helping and the Papa saved," she shrugged and held out her hands, "we will not worry over small things like a party."

The way she said it made Myrtle Albertina forget about Mrs. Andrews. It made her feel purry-warm and pleased inside. All the way back to town she felt that way, even though the day had grown hot and the way out to the Frog Pond seemed to stretch longer and longer in her mind.

She stopped at the creek to wet her face with cool water and to drink. Major drank too, but stopped suddenly to growl at a noise in the willows.

"I can see you hiding, Skinny Hooper," Myrtle Albertina called.

Skinny waded across to her. "You didn't see me at first. I've been following you all the way from town. Where's Tuley?"

She told him.

"My pop's all right. But yours isn't, is he? Too bad."

"He's going to be all right."

"That's good. Say, I heard Tuley's going away. I don't want him to."

"Neither do I."

"What's he going for?"

"Because he has to. Because of Uncle Harvey's business. Unless I find some gold."

"What's finding gold got to do with it?"

Myrtle Albertina told him what Uncle Harvey had said about Mama's necklace. "So, I'm going to try to find him some."

"You must think gold grows on trees or something."

"I do not. I know you have to dig and dig and look and look, and that's what I'm going to do, Mr. Skinny Hooper. At Papa's old Frog Pond claim."

"Hold your horses, Myrtie. Listen, are you telling me Tuley could stay if we got enough nuggets?"

"Maybe he could. If Uncle Harvey could afford to live here longer, more people could know him and see what kind of pictures he takes."

"I get it." The freckles on Skinny's nose seemed to wiggle in the sunlight. "I'll help you. Tuley's my best friend and I want him to stay in Eureka Hill more than anything. When do we dig?"

"Right now. After I go to our place to get Papa's pick."

"It's kind of hot for that kind of work today."

"I know. But we haven't much time."

Skinny sighed. "All right, then."

When they were near the house, Major ran ahead of them and up the steps, whining and scratching at the door. "He's wondering what's happened to your folks," Skinny said.

"It must be hard to be a dog and not understand things, don't you think? Come, Major." She tried to explain to him about Mama and Papa but he whined until she and Skinny found the pick and started for the woods.

The light came through the unmoving trees in long hot lines. Even the birds were quiet in the noonday heat.

"Whew," Skinny said, "I think I'll give it a try right here in the shade," and he started to dig.

Myrtle Albertina couldn't help laughing. "Oh Skinny, you know you couldn't find gold there."

"Why not?"

She giggled. "You know it's too close to the trail where the miners walk all the time."

Skinny grinned and for a few minutes made

the dirt fly in all directions. "I'm hungry," he said, handing Myrtle Albertina the pick. "I'm going to lunch."

"I'll give you half of mine."

"No, I guess not. Mom will be expecting me. Besides, I bet there's an easier way than this to get nuggets. I'll find some, Myrtie. Honest I will."

"Papa says gold is always hard to find."

"I have to go now, so g'bye. Bye, Major."

After he had gone, Myrtle Albertina stayed on the trail between the pine trees for a while, then cut across a wide flowery meadow to the Town Talk Road. Her feet felt heavy and her tummy empty, and she wondered what Mama and Papa were having for lunch.

It would be fine if they could come home before school was out. Yet as soon as they came home, Uncle Harvey would feel free to leave Eureka Hill when he was ready, which meant that Tuley . . . Yet certainly Papa could never come home too soon to please her. She sighed again and decided that feelings were very mixed-up things. How would it be, she wondered, with Tuley gone. She couldn't imagine it.

"Oh Major," she said, "we've just got to find some gold."

She tried to hurry but her pick was heavy and her lunch bag banged back and forth against her. She thought of Lupita walking this way to and from school every day. She was glad she usually had to walk only one mile—down her hill, along the lane and through the town to Bell Hill, where the school was.

The Martinez family raised chickens on their place so they would have the best for the tamales they served at their tamale parlor in town. Myrtle Albertina remembered going there with Mama and Papa once, sitting at a clean scrubbed table in a curtained booth.

Her thoughts were broken by the cackling of chickens and Major's excited barking as he started after the sound. She had to call him three times before he would come back, so she held his collar all the rest of the way to the Frog Pond.

The Frog Pond claim was really only a tunnel at the end of a gulch. The narrow track leading into it, once used by the small ore cars that brought out the gold-bearing quartz, was rusty now. She peered into the darkness, trying to see if any cars were still there, but all she could see was a thick dusty tangle of old spider webs. Papa needn't worry about her going in there.

She decided where she would dig first, then sat down in the shade to share her lunch with Major. He was more interested in playing with a horned toad than in eating. He barked all around it, sometimes almost pushing it with his nose, then, startled, leaping back. Myrtle Albertina ate her pasty, saving an end for Major, which he ate as soon as the horned toad disappeared. Then she ate her apple, stood up, stretched and started to dig.

Major tried to help by scratching and throwing dirt in a dusty cloud. "Stop, Major! You can't find gold that way. That way, you'll bury it." She threw a pine cone as far as she could, told him to fetch it and went back to her digging.

She dug for a long time. Her pick felt heavier and heavier, and her arms ached. Perspiration oozed through her hair and down her neck, and her skin felt prickly and dirty. Often she found rocks that looked as though they might hold gold, but she couldn't break them to find out. No wonder they needed such big old stamp mills at the mine, she thought.

Several times, because she was hoping so hard, she thought she saw gold. But it was always fool's gold. It was pretty and shiny enough but it wasn't worth anything at all. "Fool's gold glitters," Papa had once told her, "but real gold glows."

If I dig long enough and hard enough, she kept thinking, if I have patience . . . if I dig long enough . . . She stood up, stretched her tired body and stamped her feet to shake the dust and dirt from her shoes and stockings. She tried to brush her dress with her hands, but the dirt in her sweaty palms had changed to reddish-brown mud and made her dress messier than ever. She pushed her hair back from her burning face with one arm and was just wondering whether she could go on working when she heard every Martinez chicken break into wild squawking. She heard something else too, Major's barking.

Grabbing her pick, she ran as fast as she could across a wide expanse of tarweed to the Martinez place. "Major," she called as she ran. "Come here, Major!"

Major didn't and when she climbed the fence to look over into the chicken yard, she saw that

he couldn't. His collar was being held firmly by
a scolding girl, while all around them chickens
squawked and fluttered.

"Lupita, did he hurt any chickens?"

"Oh, hello, Myrtle Albertina. No, he didn't.
But he's scared them half to death." Lupita
laughed. "Climb over. I was in the house when
I heard the noise and I thought Major must be
at least a fox or a chicken hawk. *Ay de mí*,
you're so dirty."

"I know. I've been digging for gold. You take

89

care of the chickens, Lupita. I'll hold Major."

"Let's get out of the chicken yard. You and Major go ahead. I'll take care of the gate."

Myrtle Albertina pulled Major out of the yard and waited for Lupita to come out and close it. "Oh goodness," she said, "I'm so tired."

"Why're you digging for gold? Where's Tuley?"

"He's working for—"

"Wait. I have to hurry. To the tamale parlor to help *mía madre*. We're so busy there on Saturday nights. Come on, you can tell me as we go."

Myrtle Albertina did and, even though she was hot and tired, it seemed to her that the way back was much shorter than the going. As they turned into the sunny alley off Main Street where the tamale parlor was, the rich smells of cooking chicken and peppery sauces rushed to meet them.

"Ah, *niñita mía*," cried Mrs. Martinez when she saw Myrtle Albertina with Lupita, "how is the father?"

"He's going to be fine."

Lupita had opened a cupboard and was setting out thick white plates in even piles. "Already her Uncle Harvey's working in the mine for her father," she said.

Mrs. Martinez' face broke into smiles and she nodded. Then she dipped a corner of her apron into a pan of warm water, wiped Myrtle Albertina's face with it and started on her hands.

"Ouch," Myrtle Albertina whispered.

Mrs. Martinez turned Myrtle Albertina's hands over inside her own and frowned. "For why, *niñita mía*, why such blisters on the hands?"

Myrtle Albertina hid her hands behind her while she shyly explained what she hoped to do to keep Tuley in Eureka Hill.

"Tell your uncle this is as good place to live as any. We also, at first, thought not to stay." She hesitated. "We felt . . . how you say it, Lupita? Felt not at home. No more. Now we like it very much. The stranger must take time to become known."

"With us the tamales helped," said Lupita.

Mrs. Martinez laughed and removed the lid from a steaming pot. "True, Myrtle Albertina. First, the people like the tamales. Now I think people like the Martinez' also." She lifted a neat fat bundle from the bubbling water. "You know what makes a tamale, Myrtle Albertina?"

"I had one here once, with Mama and Papa."

"A tamale is first cornhusks laid just so, spread over with white cornmeal, more cornhusks, more cornmeal, then much chicken with sauce. Roll all up together like small pillow with strings tying in goodness at both ends." As Mrs. Martinez talked she wrapped four of them in heavy newspaper. "One for your auntie, one for uncle, one for Tuley and one for you. None for you," she told Major, shaking her finger at him.

Major did have a taste of tamale for supper though. Myrtle Albertina gave it to him and he didn't like it.

"That's because he's not a Mexican dog," Tuley said.

"I'm not a Mexican woman but *I* love them," Aunt Eva said. "Major just doesn't eat them enough to develop a taste for them, that's all."

"Mrs. Martinez told me to tell you something, Uncle Harvey. It's about staying here. In Eureka Hill."

When Myrtle Albertina had finished her telling, Tuley went to sit close to his father. "I think Mrs. Martinez is right, Father. She's a smart, jolly woman."

Uncle Harvey grinned and wiggled his eyebrows at Tuley. "If her advice is as good as her tamales, well . . . Besides, if some kind person is going to see that we're fed every day, we won't have to worry about selling pictures at all. Mary's pasties, Mrs. Hooper's saffron cake, Mrs.—"

"Father, I'm serious."

"I know you are, Son. I know just how you feel."

"Then you will think about what Mrs. Mart—"

"Tuley," Aunt Eva interrupted gently, "your father's very tired."

Uncle Harvey grinned. "Be careful of me, Son," he teased, "because I've done today just what Uncle Ed does every day. Look here," he held out his hands, "a mollycoddle with blisters."

"You are not a mollycoddle." Aunt Eva reached for his hand and held it against her cheek. "You are a very kind man."

"You are, you know, Father."

"Thank you, Tuley. Your saying that makes it doubly hard for me to ask you to do something that you won't like doing. Will you collect some boxes from the stores and help Mom-Eva with packing when she's ready? I'll do what I can at night. All right, Son? If we pack gradually we may not mind it so much."

Tuley nodded without speaking. Myrtle Albertina watched him pile the cornhusks from his tamale, edge to edge, across his plate, then muss them up and start again. She thought of Uncle Harvey's blisters and of how surprised he'd be if he knew she had some too.

"Uncle Harvey, if you had some gold, wouldn't you maybe stay?"

Uncle Harvey looked surprised. "Well now," he said, rubbing his chin, "I guess we don't have to decide about that, do we? You haven't, by chance, found us a treasure?"

CHAPTER 7

Time Flying

MYRTLE ALBERTINA had always liked Sundays for many reasons. Papa didn't have to go to work, they all dressed up and went to church when the church bells rang and people took time to visit or stroll. With Mama and Papa away, Sunday still seemed special, and, as it turned out, it was.

On the way to church, Myrtle Albertina and the others met Madame La Rue. She rushed up to them on Church Street and said she hoped what she'd heard wasn't true—that they were thinking of going away.

Myrtle Albertina watched Aunt Eva's face for an answer but it didn't come. "Madame La Rue," she said instead, "I want you to meet my husband."

Madame La Rue held out her hand and Un-

cle Harvey took it and bowed. "I may be un-
known to you, Mr. Stevens," she teased, "but
you are not to me. To me, Myrtle Albertina has
told much, singing your praise."

Uncle Harvey's face turned very red. "Thank
you. Thank you very much. But you know you
mustn't believe everything you hear."

"I believe everything." Madame La Rue gathered her full long skirts in one hand, looked at
Uncle Harvey for a moment with her eyes
sparkling then winked at Myrtle Albertina and
went on her way.

"Well," breathed Uncle Harvey, grinning.

Aunt Eva laughed and took his arm. "When
you come down from the clouds, Mr. Stevens,
I'll be here, waiting."

"Me too, Father."

"Me too, Uncle Harvey."

Myrtle Albertina and Tuley giggled so hard
right up to the church door that Aunt Eva had to
shush them, but she was almost giggling herself.

After church, they walked slowly home along
Main Street. The sunlight falling through Aunt
Eva's ruffled pink parasol made her look so

pretty that Myrtle Albertina wished she had
brought hers too. Only hers was blue.

"Look," Tuley whispered. "There's Mrs. Andrews and Kit Carson."

Mrs. Andrews stood in front of the hotel with
her cat in her arms. She was talking in a lively
way to a little group of people but when she
looked up and saw Uncle Harvey and his family
coming, she stopped. Myrtle Albertina could
almost feel the sudden silence as they passed.
The ladies nodded and the men took off their
hats but not a word was spoken until Mrs. Andrews called after them, "Any news from your
folks, Myrtle Albertina?"

Myrtle Albertina turned. "No, Mrs. Andrews,
not yet."

"They're pretty stuck-up, looking at us like
that," Tuley burst out as they turned the corner
into their street.

"Oh, come now, Son. You want everybody to
be as charming and flattering to us as Madame La Rue?"

"They were probably talking about the cave-
in," Aunt Eva said. "Most everybody is."

Everybody was still talking about it at school
the next morning.

Skinny started it. "I was there when they brought the men out."

Lupita shuddered. "What happened then?"

"I bet Skinny wasn't there at all," Ray Harris said.

"I was too. They brought Myrtie's father first because he was hurt. I saw him."

Annette's eyes opened wide. "Could he see you?"

"Sure. He said, 'Hello, Skinny.'" He shrugged. "I'm lucky because my pop wasn't hurt. But Myrtle Albertina's lucky too, in a way."

"Skinny Hooper, how can you say that?" Ruby Pearl, who was usually so quiet, flushed and ran to put her arm through Myrtle Albertina's.

Skinny laughed. "You don't have to get so mad. I only meant she's got a swell uncle who's gone to work at the Red Dog for her dad."

"Oh," said Ruby Pearl.

"He's no other," Skinny shouted, "than the husband of Miss Eva *and* the father of old Tuley here."

Tuley looked proud and started to turn somersaults. Skinny joined him and soon every boy

in the schoolyard except Gong Tong was doing it.

Gong Tong, who was much older, stood slim and smiling, holding his books and watching while the girls, giggling and squealing, ran around pretending to get in the boys' way.

Only Ruby Pearl, Thelma Wing, a new girl, whose family had just moved into rooms over the grocery store, and Myrtle Albertina didn't run. Myrtle Albertina would have but suddenly, as she watched Tuley showing gladness for what Skinny had said about his father, she felt very lonely for her own. She decided to go home right after school to see if there was word from Mama instead of digging again for gold.

There was a letter, a small one. It was stuck under the door and the envelope said, "To Myrtle Albertina Martin, kindness of Dr. Dunn." Myrtle Albertina ran into Uncle Harvey's studio, opened it and read:

> Hello Darling—
> I'm glad to tell you Papa's break is a clean one which is surely a blessing. His head is also better. More news soon. Don't grow too fast while we're away but do have fun.
> Love, Mother

She sat down on the big throne chair and read the note again. She felt good and still inside, like saying thank you, God, over and over again. Now that I know Papa's *really* getting better, she thought, I'll look for gold again tomorrow.

But she didn't. Or the next day or the next. Living in her new home was so interesting that it was hard to think of anything else. Since Uncle Harvey's place was just around the corner from Main Street and close to both the livery stable and the firehouse, something was usually happening. When it wasn't, Myrtle Albertina and Tuley gathered grass for the livery stable horses or wandered around to the back street to visit Ray Harris' father's blacksmith shop. Often they played street games with their friends— Hop Scotch, Follow the Leader, Run Sheep Run or Pretending.

Before Myrtle Albertina realized it several weeks had slipped by and suddenly it was June. Even then she might have gone on telling herself there was still plenty of time to find gold if it hadn't been for another letter from Mama. Dr. Dunn had brought it by after early Sunday supper.

Dearest Chick—

We hope we can see you soon. Our days drag without you. Isn't it strange that while time seems endless to us, it's probably flying for you and will, until Tuley goes away . . .

"Goes away." Holding the letter she sat by the open window watching a robin tilting on a branch of the tree of heaven. Goes away. Once again she tried to picture Tuley living somewhere else and this time she could. The train carries people away every single day, she thought, and it can carry Tuley too. She imagined Tuley waving to her from the back of a fast-moving coach and she sighed deeply. She cushioned her head in her arms on the windowsill and promised herself to go to work, harder than she'd ever worked before. Even if it meant more blisters, more dirt. Still, she thought, there was no use wasting time at the Frog Pond if there was no gold there. There certainly hadn't seemed to be. Perhaps she'd be luckier at panning the streams.

She remembered an old framed photograph in the newspaper office. It showed a quart measure of gold dust which had been panned out of Rabbit Creek during the month of May in 1851. She became so busy dreaming about gold that she scarcely noticed the evening come. She even wondered where she could find a quart measure, then giggled at herself for being so silly. As if she could ever find a quart of gold. But if she could fill her pocket . . . half-fill it . . . just fill it enough to make it feel a little heavy . . .

"Myrtle Alber . . . tina!" Tuley's voice bounced into her thoughts so suddenly that she jumped, then leaned out the window and waved.

"Come out," he called, "some of the kids are here to play Castle and Moat."

Myrtle Albertina went to the front porch and stood there peering through the dusk. "Who's there?"

"Lupita and . . ."

"Thelma's here, too," Skinny's voice interrupted, "and Ray Harris and me."

"And Major." Laughing, Myrtle Albertina ran to join them.

Castle and Moat was a game she and Tuley had invented to fit the big grassy hump in the vacant lot at the end of the street. It had once been a pile of loose red dirt dug up by gold seekers, but now it was a green mound surrounded by a shallow trench. The mound was the castle, the trench the moat. The drawbridge was a long board. The prince and princess, to avoid capture, could move the drawbridge from one place across the moat to another or they could shake it or rock it or tip it. If, after ten tries, the knights hadn't succeeded in crossing

103

the moat, the prince and princess were victorious.

"First," announced Skinny, "Tuley and Myrtie can be prince and princess and we'll be the knights in armor and I'll bet we capture them fast. You tell 'em the rules, Tuley."

As Tuley explained, Myrtle Albertina, longing to start the game, shivered and hugged herself with excitement. With faces only dimly seen through the gathering shadows, everything seemed mysterious and real.

"As soon as we've won, Lupita and I will be prince and princess," Skinny shouted.

"All right. Remember, you can only cross on the drawbridge." Tuley swung away from them, dropped the board and cried, "The drawbridge is down. Go!"

Running, laughing, panting, they shouted and scolded back and forth to each other. Over and over Tuley and Myrtle Albertina lowered the drawbridge, waited for a knight to step on it, then raised or rocked it to send him rolling in the grass. They did it five times . . . six . . . seven . . .

"Eight down and two to go," yelled Tuley.

"Prince, look out! Drawbridge up!" cried

Myrtle Albertina. "It's Knight Lupita again!"

"Up she goes," Tuley panted and Lupita stumbled backward, shrieking and giggling.

"Nine down and one to go."

"No, you don't," Skinny shouted. "You're captured. I swam the moat."

"You can't," Myrtle Albertina said, "a moat has high steep sides."

"Well, I did."

"Anyway," Tuley said, "it's against the rules."

"Ah, come on back, Skinny," Ray called, "and play the game right. We'll win next time."

"They're already captured, I tell you. Come on."

"If he wants to break the rules," Tuley whispered to Myrtle Albertina, "let's escape."

Before Skinny or the others knew what was happening, Tuley dropped the board away from where the knights were standing and ran across it into the dusk with Myrtle Albertina and Major following close behind.

"We will escape you villains," Tuley called back in his deepest voice.

"Forever," Myrtle Albertina cried.

They heard Skinny start after them, then the

others, all calling, "Get them! Get them!" and
they ran faster. They waited, listening, in the
great black shade of the blacksmith shop, ducked
into an alley, crept along the shadows to cross
Main Street into another alley and dashed past
the brightly lightly tamale parlor into the darkness of the trees along the creek.

There they stopped, gasping for breath, listening. All they could hear was Major gulping
a drink from the creek and they giggled.

"Do you think we've lost them?" whispered
Myrtle Albertina.

"I think we lost them right away. I bet they
thought we'd run away from town instead of
through it, don't you?"

"What shall we do now?"

"Wait here, I guess. Till they give up and go
home."

She felt around for a cozy place to sit under
the willows and pulled Major to sit by her.
"There's room for you, too, Tuley."

"I'd better stand guard. What's that?" He
parted the willows and looked out but the only
sounds were the shrilling of crickets and the
flow of the creek.

"Tuley, look how the stars are hanging in the trees."

"Uh huh."

"I'm going to pan for gold after school tomorrow. Will you go with me?"

"I can't tomorrow, or the next day. I promised to help Mom-Eva with packing. But I can go Wednesday if you want."

"All right. But I haven't very much time. So I'll go tomorrow, too."

"Time for what?"

"Oh, Tuley, you know! To find gold for Uncle Harvey. So you won't have to go."

Tuley pretended to groan. "Myrtle Albertina, I bet you're the stubbornest little old girl in the whole world. But I like you. I like you very much." Turning, he pulled her to her feet. "Come on. Let's go home."

CHAPTER 8

One Nugget

THE NEXT DAY Myrtle Albertina asked each of her girl friends if they could go panning with her after school. But each one had to go right home so she sighed and asked Skinny.

"No, because I'm going with Tuley. To help him carry boxes. Besides," he looked around to make sure that no one was listening and whispered, "I told you I'd get some gold."

"I know you did. But right now you're helping them get ready to go."

"Oh, hold your horses, Myrtie. I'm just helping Tuley for fun. I made you a promise and I'll keep it. Honest I will."

So she and Major set out again, alone.

At home, where she stopped for Papa's pan, she was surprised to see that the climbing rose over the front porch had burst, almost over-

109

night, into pink blooming. If only Mama could see it, she thought, while it's so beautiful. If only she and Papa could come home soon, and if only, when they did come, she could tell them Tuley was staying. Papa would be pretty surprised that she'd been able to find gold after all.

"The world is deep and high and wide . . ." she sang, thinking this was her own song and she'd almost forgotten it. Before she had sung it through, though, she was starting another. "I'll pan and I'll pan for nuggets of gold . . . as great big as beans and glowing as . . . buttercups."

Buttercups splashed all over the meadow at the edge of the forest. They brushed her shoe-tops as she stepped through them, singing, to where Rabbit Creek ran noisily, glittering and swirling over the rocks.

She knelt, dipping her face to drink, and Major drank, splashing, beside her. "Major!" She started to scold but had to laugh instead. "Do you always have to drink where I do?"

Major picked up a stick and started to prance.

"Mr. Show-off," she said and he pranced more than ever. He ran through the water, leaped over rocks and sniffed behind bushes. Then he seemed to catch an exciting scent and raced away barking into the woods.

She drank again and went to work. Scooping a mixture of sandy rock and water into her pan, she shook and rocked it to let any gold sink to the bottom. Then she slowly poured the water off as she'd seen panners do. Over and over again she scooped, shook, rocked and poured. But she found no gold.

She stretched herself and walked farther upstream, searching for a lucky place. Once a spotted fawn bounding away into the brush startled her so that she slipped on the wet rocks in the creek. But she caught herself and went on.

The shadows of the trees grew longer. The water, catching at a low branch of alder, made a secret sucking sound. She called Major and, kneeling, went to work again. Her braids dragged in the water as she leaned forward and she had to keep tossing them back. Wishing, wishing hard for a nugget, she made her eyes examine every inch of rocky sand in the pan.

The late sun made dizzy, swirly patterns in

the water and her hands felt spongy with wetness. Scoop, shake, rock, scoop, shake. She sighed and scooped again, trying hard not to be discouraged. Then one braid fell forward and when she tried, impatiently, to throw it back, she slipped and went plunging into the creek, pan and all. Gasping and angry, she scrambled out, felt a long shadow fall over her and looked up into the merry eyes of Big Joe.

"Ed's girl wet as drowned cat. Come to campoody."

"I can't now, Big Joe. I have to work."

He shook his head and looked stern. "Too wet. Ed not like. Come."

She sighed again and followed him, her wet shoes sloshing, her skirts dripping and dragging around her legs.

"Isn't there any gold left in Rabbit Creek, Big Joe?"

"Hard to find."

"But I tried hard."

"Kids can't find." Big Joe shrugged, then turned to look at her. His eyes in his brown face were solemn. "You need gold? Ed in hospital. He need?"

112

"I don't think so. Because Uncle Harvey's working for him. I need it for Uncle Harvey."

Big Joe didn't seem to understand. He frowned, shook his head and turned from the creek trail to a narrower one that led through the trees. During the whole winding way to the campoody, Myrtle Albertina couldn't think of another word to say.

Big Joe's home was made of long strips of wood laid over each other. It looked like a wigwam except that it had a real doorway, like a house. Mrs. Joe sat in front of it on the ground, but when Big Joe pointed to Myrtle Albertina and walked away, she scrambled to her feet.

The full skirt of her dark dress dragged over the pine needles and a red handkerchief, pulled over her head and tied under her chin, framed her round brown face. She smiled shyly as she took hold of Myrtle Albertina, unfastened her dress and, pulling it off, squeezed the water out of it and hung it from a tree.

Myrtle Albertina, feeling very bare, shivered in her petticoats. "Where's Young Joe?" she asked.

"Cut wood." His mother pointed toward the

forest and laughingly removed the wet petticoats also. Then she dived inside her home and
came out with a faded calico dress which she
slipped over Myrtle Albertina's head. It covered her like a bag all the way to her ankles and
the sleeves were so long she couldn't see her
hands.

Mrs. Joe looked so pleased at what she'd done

that Myrtle Albertina had to smile. But what she was thinking was how to get home without being seen looking so terrible.

"Thank you very much, Mrs. Joe. I have to go now. Good-by." At the edge of the clearing she turned and waved and Mrs. Joe waved back.

As soon as she was out of sight of the campoody she held the dress up with both hands and tried to run. The way home seemed very long. The sun sank golden behind the pines and evening crept into the woods.

"Ma . . . jor," she called and then remembered. Her meeting with Big Joe had made her forget that Major was with her. He must have lost her trail. Probably, she thought, he's home by now. Clutching her dress even higher, she ran out of the woods, down the hill, across the creek and, keeping close to the shadows of the poplar trees, turned into Mill Street.

A man was standing in front of the firehouse but he didn't even look up as she dashed to Uncle Harvey's, around the house and up the back steps.

"Hello, everybody," she cried, throwing open the door, then laughed because Major was leaping on her before she could close it.

"He's—" Aunt Eva started to say, then cried out, "Goodness gracious, my darling, where have you been?"

"How *do* you do, Miss Martin." Uncle Harvey covered his mouth to hide his smiles and Tuley pretended to faint.

Then he cried, "Ladies and gentlemen, here we see the latest style for the year 1891."

"Oh Tuley, you're silly. I fell in the creek, that's all. And Big Joe saw me and said I was too wet so he took me to his campoody and—"

"You know him, this Indian?" Uncle Harvey, suddenly frowning, interrupted.

"Of course she does, Father. Big Joe's a friend of Uncle Ed's. His son is Young Joe and he's a friend of ours."

"I see," said Uncle Harvey.

"If you could only see how you look, Pet." Aunt Eva shook with laughter as she pulled Myrtle Albertina into her arms.

"When did Major come?"

"Just a few minutes ago. We couldn't believe you weren't with him."

"I lost him and then I guess he lost me."

Tuley grinned. "I bet you felt funny coming home in a big dress like that."

Myrtle Albertina giggled.

"Better to look funny than to catch cold," Aunt Eva said. "And that's probably what Mrs. Joe thought, too. Come have a bath, Myrtle Albertina. Right now."

Later, as they were eating supper, Tuley asked, "Anybody want to know what happened to me today?"

"We certainly do, Son."

"When I went to Van Metre's for a packing box, Mr. Van Metre teased me. He thought I wanted it for a doghouse or something, I guess. I told him we needed it for packing and he said, 'Tell your father we need a photographer in this town.'"

Aunt Eva, about to cut a chocolate cake, stopped with her knife in the air and Uncle Harvey wiggled his eyebrows at Tuley.

"They *do*, too, Father."

Uncle Harvey pulled the table drawer open and took out his old appointment book, the one he had shown Papa. "I'm afraid, Son," he said, "that this speaks louder than words."

"But Father, maybe—"

The knock on the door was such a quiet one that they all listened, wondering if they had really heard it. Even Major listened. Then the door opened and Young Joe stood there, shy and unsmiling, with Myrtle Albertina's dress and petticoats in his hand.

"Hello, Young Joe," cried Tuley, "come on in."

"Thank you, Young Joe," said Myrtle Albertina as she took her clothes.

"Come," Aunt Eva said, "have some cake."

"Sure," Tuley urged, "have some with us."

Still Young Joe hesitated. Then, swift as a deer, he dashed into the room and pressed something into Uncle Harvey's hand. "Big Joe send," he said and, before they could stop him, he was gone.

Myrtle Albertina grabbed the dress she had worn home, Tuley took a piece of cake and they ran after him. "Young Joe, wait. Please."

He waited outside the glow of the livery-stable light. Even in the shadow they could see his smile as he took what they brought him and slipped away in the darkness.

For a moment they looked after him, then dashed back into the house to find Aunt Eva and Uncle Harvey bending over something in his outstretched hand. Uncle Harvey moved closer to the lamplight and when he looked up at them his eyes were full of surprise. "What do you make of this, Myrtle Albertina?" he asked.

"Golly, Myrtle Albertina, look," breathed Tuley.

There on Uncle Harvey's palm was a scrap of red calico and on the calico was a nugget. It was a small one, not nearly as big as a bean, but as soon as Myrtle Albertina saw it, she clapped her hands.

Aunt Eva smiled. "Myrtle Albertina seems to know what it's all about."

"It's a nugget for Uncle Harvey from Big Joe, that's all."

"But why?" Uncle Harvey exclaimed. "He doesn't even know me. So I can't understand . . ."

"He knows Papa." Myrtle Albertina looked at their puzzled faces and giggled. "Don't you see, Uncle Harvey, it's your first nugget. Because you need it, I guess."

"I need it?"

"Of course, Uncle Harvey. So you can stay in Eureka Hill."

CHAPTER 9

Carrot Gold

D R. DUNN called early the next morning before Myrtle Albertina and Tuley had had breakfast. He knocked on the door and came in smiling, asking Aunt Eva if she could give a poor hard-working doctor a cup of tea.

"Indeed I can, Dr. Dunn," Aunt Eva answered gaily. "Sit down here with Myrtle Albertina and Tuley."

"Did you come to tell us we could go to see Papa and Mama, Dr. Dunn?"

"I came to tell you they're about ready to come home. They did say, though, they'd been expecting to see you."

"And we've been expecting to see them." Aunt Eva gave him a cup of tea. "But with the last of school and packing and . . . well, anyway, Harvey's arranged with the livery stable for us to go Thursday evening."

"Goody," cried Myrtle Albertina.

"Will that be soon enough, Dr. Dunn?" Tuley asked.

"I think so, lad. I think they can hold out for another day or so." He chuckled and took a great drink of tea. "Ah, deee . . . licious!"

"I guess it seems a little silly to drive all the way to Gold Town when we'll be seeing Mary and Ed here soon. But we did promise and the arrangements are made."

"And besides, we want to go, don't we, Tuley?" Myrtle Albertina jumped up from the table. "I've waited and waited and waited, and now I don't want to wait another minute. I wish we could go today, or tomorrow anyway. And I wish we could go right after school. That's what I wish."

"I thought you had to look for gold after school," teased Tuley. "You going to stop working on it now? Just because Father's got a nugget?"

"Of course not, Mr. Tuley." She pretended to pull his hair. "You know we need more gold than that."

Carrot Gold

"What's this about gold?" Dr. Dunn asked but before anyone could answer him the kitchen clock started to strike.

"Oh my," he cried and, jumping to his feet, he gulped the rest of his tea. "Eight o'clock and I'm supposed to be in Gold Town at half past. Thanks for the tea, Eva. Come, Myrtle Albertina, walk to my buggy with me. Now," he asked as they walked to the gate, "what's all this about gold?"

"We need some."

Dr. Dunn laughed so hard that his patient little horse tossed her head. "I guess most of us do, Myrtle Albertina."

"Well I've been looking and digging and . . ."

He took the reins and climbed into the buggy. "Listen, young lady," he said, leaning toward her, "there's only one sure way to get gold *or* money these days. And that's by working at a real job. Your dad gets paid for mining, your uncle for taking pictures."

"But he—"

"And I, for trying to make sick people well. It's true, my pay is sometimes a cord of wood or a fat chicken but oftener it's a nugget, a little gold dust or, best of all, good old gold or silver coins. So, if you want gold, Myrtle Albertina, you'd best wait till you're old enough to earn it." He snapped the reins and threw her a kiss.

She turned toward the house, stopped at the gate, and stood on it, thinking. She went on thinking and swinging for a long time, until Aunt Eva and Tuley came out with books and lunch pails, ready for school. By lunchtime she had made up her mind to get a job. After school she told Tuley about it.

"I'm going to try to work for Ah Sam."

"I thought we were going panning tomorrow."

"If I can get a nugget for doing work, then . . . I guess I'll have to go anyway, though, to get Papa's pan. But today, I'll . . ."

"What can you do for Ah Sam?"

"Oh, something, I bet. It's no use asking for a job at stores because I'm too young. Besides I like Ah Sam's garden."

"Golly, I should think you've got enough to think about with so much happening at once. What do you want to work for?"

"As if you didn't know!"

"Oh, you!" Tuley shook his head. "All right, give me your books. I'll take them home for you." He grinned. "Better give me your lunch pail, too, unless you need it for carrying your pay."

She made a face at him, waved and turned from the road to the creek path. She followed its winding way in and out through sun-splashed poplars, clumps of trees of heaven and the small falling-down shacks which Chinese miners had used in the early days. When she reached the bridge leading into the Chinese gardens, she saw Ah Sam's wife coming toward her.

Mrs. Ah Sam wasn't much bigger than Myrtle Albertina and just as slender. Her glossy black hair was pulled straight back into smooth coils held by golden combs. She wore a black silk coat and trousers and walked stiffly on her tiny feet (lily feet, people called them) in their dainty doll shoes.

"How do you do, Mrs. Ah Sam."

"Hi yo," Mrs. Ah Sam answered in her high sweet voice. She smiled, ducked her head a little as she passed Myrtle Albertina, and went on.

Myrtle Albertina crossed the bridge and knocked on the first of the cabins. The door was open and she could see inside openings too, leading from one room to another. She could

see, even without peeking, a corner of a red-
silk hanging embroidered in gold, and a huge
black, carved chest. She could smell the pleasant strangeness of incense. When no one came
she knocked again, then walked slowly toward
the gardens.

Ah Sam was crouched over a wooden platform built around a spring, washing vegetables.
"Good day, missy," he called.

"Good day, Ah Sam."

Ah Sam went on working. Beyond him in the
sunlight she could see Gong Tong in blue work
clothes, bent over new green plants with a hoe
in his hand. She could still smell the incense,
mixed now with a minty smell from the grass
and the earthy one from the freshly pulled carrots and turnips.

Suddenly she felt herself getting bashful so
she spoke quickly. "Can I do a job for you,
please, Ah Sam?"

He smiled and shook his head.

"I would like very much to help you."

"Very dirty for hands."

"I don't mind, Ah Sam. Because I want to
earn something."

"Oh, so?" He chuckled.

126

"I know I can help you if you'll show me how."

He motioned for her to kneel beside him over the spring, briskly rubbed some dirty carrots between his hands in the water, shook them and threw them on the pile already washed.

She tried to do the same and looked up at him. He nodded, handed her more carrots and they worked on together. He worked much faster than she, yet seemed to see everything. He saw that one of her turnips was rotten and threw it away. He saw his yellow cat ready to spring at a bird and clapped his hands. He showed her a tiny green frog flattened against the damp wood at the side of the platform. He pointed to a horsehair snake in the spring. It was such a hair-sized thing that she couldn't see it at all till it swam, wiggling across her own reflection.

She became so interested she almost forgot that what she was doing was work. Even when a woman came to buy some cabbages and onions and Ah Sam went to get them for her, Myrtle Albertina went right on working.

When Ah Sam returned and saw how much she had done, he showed her how to tie the

washed vegetables into bunches with strips of tough reed.

After she had tied for a while she stopped to stretch. Ah Sam smiled at her, his quick hands busy.

"Do you ever have trouble, Ah Sam?"

Ah Sam finished tying a bunch of carrots before he answered. "Same all people. Sometimes trouble, sometimes not."

She thought about that while a blue dragon-
fly dipped over the water and zoomed up into
the sunlight. "Most of the time for me, it's not,"
she said, starting to wash turnips.

"Papa better?"

"Yes. He's getting so well he can come home.
My trouble's about Tuley. You remember Tuley,
don't you, Ah Sam? He has to go away because
Uncle Harvey's business isn't good."

Ah Sam looked sorry but went on working

without saying anything. So did she. But speaking of Tuley had made her remember what she was working for and now she could think of little else. She tried to work faster and faster as the sun sank lower and lower.

The mine whistles blew for quitting time and Gong Tong came in from the fields. He greeted her quietly and washed his hands in the spring. His mother came from town and spoke rapidly in laughing Chinese to him and Ah Sam. Then she smiled at Myrtle Albertina and went into the cabin and Gong Tong went with her.

"Enough when turnips finished," Ah Sam said and followed them.

The late afternoon became very still except for the singing of insects and the murmuring of voices from the cabins. Myrtle Albertina sighed. She was quite ready now to go home. The yellow cat brushed against her leg and she stopped to pet him, then hurried to finish.

She wondered how much Papa earned in one day. Or the doctor? Or how much work equaled one nugget. She tied the last of the turnips and washed her hands. She was drying them on her petticoat when Ah Sam came out.

"Time now go home," he said and handed her

a large bundle wrapped in a Chinese newspaper. "Many carrots for good work. Also presents for Tuley family."

She took the carrots and for one long disappointed moment, could think of nothing to say. Then she felt Ah Sam's steady eyes watching her and she looked up. "Thank you very much, Ah Sam. It was fun working for you." All her rushing way home she knew that was really true.

When she softly opened the kitchen door, Major bounded to meet her and lick her hand.

"Hey," said Tuley, looking up from his geography book, "what's all that you're lugging? Did you work?"

She set the bundle down, tugged at the reed that held it together and carrots spilled out all over the table, carrots and three fat paper bags.

Aunt Eva put her hand to her head. "*Now*, what in the world . . . ?"

"Ah Sam said the bags are for you." Myrtle Albertina handed one to each and watched their surprised faces as they opened them.

Aunt Eva pulled a small square package, wrapped in soft red paper with Chinese writing on it, from her bag. "It's tea, the very finest."

"See what I've got," Uncle Harvey exclaimed. "My favorite preserved ginger."

"Look at mine." Tuley's hands were full of knobby brown, ball-like objects. "Say, what are these things, Myrtle Albertina? Some kind of nugget?" he teased.

"They're lichee nuts, silly. They taste much better than gold."

Tuley broke the thin shell, took out something that looked like a giant raisin and tasted, a lick at first, before he popped it into his mouth. "Uhmmm."

"Are you very sure," Uncle Harvey asked, "that Ah Sam meant these for us?"

Myrtle Albertina nodded. "Of course."

"But why?"

"Because . . ." She hesitated, frowning. She hadn't really thought why. "I guess it's because of feeling like friends to you, or something."

Uncle Harvey took a deep breath, grinned at Aunt Eva and shook his head.

"Ah Sam's been our friend for years and years, hasn't he, Aunt Eva? Mama always bakes him a cake for Chinese New Year and he always gives us lichee nuts and Chinese candy for Christmas, doesn't he?"

"That's right." Aunt Eva tossed the carrots into a bowl. "And speaking of gifts, Dr. Dunn left a chicken for us this afternoon. My, these carrots are fresh and good. I think I'll boil some right now for our supper."

Tuley cracked another lichee nut, handed one to Myrtle Albertina and went back to his geography book. "It says here that San Francisco's a great seaport. Father says you can see ships from all over the world in the harbor. And you can ride on horsecars too."

Myrtle Albertina turned away and went to sit on the floor beside Major. She still felt that something about getting carrots from Ah Sam was better than nuggets. But they couldn't keep anyone from going away. She dropped her head against Major's back and let the tears come.

In an instant Tuley was beside her. "What's the matter?" he whispered.

She shook her head.

"Tell me."

"I want to see Mama and Papa . . . and you're going to San Francisco . . . and I've tried and tried to get gold for Uncle Harvey and . . ."

"What's that?" exclaimed Uncle Harvey.

"I know it sounds crazy, Father. But it's true. She's been looking for gold for you, digging old Frog Pond, panning Rabbit Creek, and today working for Ah Sam."

Uncle Harvey rubbed his chin and looked puzzled. "Come here, Myrtle Albertina." He pulled her between his knees and lifted her chin so he could look at her. "I'd like to know why you think gold is so important to me."

She rubbed her eyes on her sleeve. "Because . . ."

"Because what?"

"You said if you had nuggets like the ones in Mama's necklace you could stay in Eureka Hill."

"Did *I* say that?"

"You certainly did, Harvey," Aunt Eva said.

"And Father, she's been talking about nuggets for you ever since."

"Well, what do you know about that?" Uncle Harvey gave her a squeeze and his face broke into smiles. "I thought you knew I was teasing about your mother's necklace, honey. Why, nuggets aren't the important things to me at all."

"What are, Father?"

"Friends, Son, for one thing. Like Myrtle Albertina here."

"Just the same," cried Tuley, "I bet you'd like some nuggets too."

"Listen, Tuley. I would like very much to have you understand something."

"What, Father?"

"Just this. Give me enough appointments in my old appointment book to keep me busy and to support us all and, believe me, I'll be glad to let somebody else have the nuggets."

CHAPTER 10

Major Chases a Deer

MYRTLE ALBERTINA dreamed of carrots. Then she turned over and dreamed of carrots again. Sometimes she was washing them, sometimes trying to catch them as they hopped and danced away out of reach, but when they fell over her like rain, she cried out and woke herself.

Already it was day with pale sunlight sliding in through the shutters. Wednesday, she thought . . . going with Tuley to Rabbit Creek this afternoon . . . one more day before going to Gold Town to see Mama and Papa . . . three more days till the end of school . . . five or six till Mama and Papa come home . . . seven or eight till Tuley goes away.

She flopped over and punched the pillow. "No, no, no." She burrowed back under the covers, thinking. Thinking. Thinking down all the little side streets of her mind to find a new idea for trying to keep Tuley. No use talking. No use looking for gold. Uncle Harvey had made that quite clear. She started to punch the pillow again but caught her breath instead and lay very, very still.

After a while she stretched and sat up, hugging her knees. Why, she wondered, hadn't she had this thought before? It was the very best one of all. She would take Uncle Harvey's appointment book and go from door to door. She remembered once, when she was eight, going from house to house trying to sell a magazine. The boy or girl who sold the most subscriptions was to win a Shetland pony free. She had worked for three afternoons and had collected eleven subscriptions.

Of course she hadn't won the pony or even the smallest prize that time. But this would be different. This would be arranging. Arranging appointments for Uncle Harvey. And I won't tell a single person, she promised herself, in case someone might not think it's a wonderful idea. Not even Tuley.

She jumped out of bed, planning. Since she was going to Rabbit Creek with Tuley this afternoon, she couldn't start till tomorrow. A shiver of excitement ran like a cold finger along her backbone and she could hardly wait to begin.

At breakfast she pulled the drawer of the kitchen table quickly, out and in, then bent her head over her cereal bowl to hide her smile. Uncle Harvey's appointment book was there.

"Let's play Hare and Hound this afternoon," Tuley said. "After we've found the pan. You think it's in Rabbit Creek?"

"I hope so. Papa wouldn't like to lose it."

They found it wedged between the rocks just a little downstream from where Myrtle Albertina had dropped it. Tuley crossed the stream on the rocks and jerked it loose. "I guess I'll try my luck," he said and scooped.

While he panned, Major ran and barked and chased squirrels and Myrtle Albertina sat, deep in thought, scarcely watching either of them. Nuggets no longer seemed very important to her compared to a list of promises to have pictures taken.

"Whew." Tuley rubbed his arm across his forehead. "I bet there never was any gold in this old stream."

"There was too," she said, laughing. "There's a picture in the *Morning News* office that proves it, a whole quart measure of gold."

"Whoever found it didn't leave even a crumb for anyone else, I guess. Come on. Let's play Hare and Hound. Before I go away I want to see if you have enough sense to stay away from mountain lions."

"Oh, you!" She wrinkled her nose at him. "You can be the hare this time, then I'll wait with Major." She called Major. She called him again. Tuley called too.

"Say, Myrtle Albertina, I haven't heard him for a while. Have you?"

"I don't remember because I was thinking about something else. Maj . . . or!"

They searched and called for a long time. "Where do you 'spose he is?"

"Gone home, I guess," Tuley said. "The way he did when you were at the campoody."

"I bet he has."

All the way home she felt sure she would find him there but she didn't. No one had seen him.

"Let's not worry about a smart dog like Major," Uncle Harvey said. "He's likely flushed a deer and is chasing him all the way to the next county."

"I saw a spotted deer near Rabbit Creek the other day."

"You see . . ."

"And, Father, if he treed a raccoon he might stay by the tree for a long time waiting for it to come down."

"Sure he might."

"There," Aunt Eva said, "nothing to worry about."

So Myrtle Albertina didn't. She didn't even worry about Tuley, when he dashed out without her. He was back again in half an hour. She thought over her plans for the next afternoon, thought of going to see Papa and Mama, studied her reading lesson and got sleepy. She didn't worry at all until morning.

She woke early, dressed and tiptoed out of the house, looking everywhere around. Sunbeams slid over leaves and rode on grasses as she walked through the new morning looking for Major. She looked for him, calling softly, all the ways they had taken yesterday—up the hill, through the woods, along the creek and back over the fields, to her own home.

She ran up the back steps to look at his bed by the well. His blanket was neat and undisturbed so she went slowly back down the steps and around to the front gate, trying not to think of the big loneliness she felt. Now, all our family are apart, she thought. When she looked up it seemed that even their house looked strange. It had a secret waiting look and the windows with their blinds down were like closed eyes peeking.

Then she remembered. She was going to be with Mama and Papa, this very night. Some of her good feelings rushed back so fast she almost laughed. She felt like running and ran fast all the way down to the bridge.

"Hey, Myrtle Albertina, wait a minute." Tuley caught up with her. "I've been looking for you and Major. Where've you been?"

"Looking too. Everywhere. Where can he be?"

Tuley shook his head. "Come on. Mom-Eva's waiting breakfast for you. When we get to school I'll tell everyone Major's missing and I'll bet we find a clue."

142

That's just what he did. He interrupted a ring game just as they were singing, "King William was King James' son and all the royal races run," and before they could go on with "upon his breast he wore a star to point the way to the candy store."

"Hey, listen to me, everybody," he shouted. "Remember Major? Myrtle Albertina's dog? Well, he's missing. Be on the lookout for him." Then he went to each person. "Skinny, Major's been gone since yesterday . . . Have you seen him around the Chinese Gardens, Gong Tong? . . . Ruby Pearl, will you tell your father to ask the people who come in his store? . . . Annette! Stop jumping a minute and listen. Major's a medium-sized dog with . . ."

"I know Major, silly." She tossed her rope around him but he sprang and freed himself.

"All right, then, look for him. Everybody, look for him."

"And that means you, and you, and you," cried Skinny, pointing. "Don't you worry, Myrtie, I'll find him for you."

Listening to them so cheered Myrtle Albertina that she decided to carry out her plans for the afternoon. If only she could get away from Tuley.

But Tuley got away from her. He said he had something important to do and he didn't say what it was. She didn't exactly like that either but she was too full of her secret to think much about it. Running all the way to the little house on Mill Street so she could get there before Aunt Eva, she left her books, grabbed Uncle Harvey's appointment book and dashed out the back way.

She hurried around the stable and along the lane to the far side of town. There she stopped before a neat yellow house behind a picket fence and decided to get started. As she went slowly up the path to the porch she felt like giggling and running away at the same time.

An old man answered her knock.

"Oh, hello, Mr. Fuller. I didn't know you lived here."

"You didn't, huh? Well, here I be. Me and my dog and that's about all. Coming in?"

"No thank you. I want to know if you'd like to have your picture taken."

"Me?" Mr. Fuller burst out laughing. He laughed so hard he shook all over and had to lean against the doorway. "Myrtle Albertina, you'll be the death of me. That's a real good joke. A picture of me!" He slapped his knee and went off again, laughing.

She laughed too. "Maybe a picture of your dog, then. That would be a good idea."

"No, I guess not. Daisy, she's my dog, and me, well, we're too old for that stuff, honey. Give my best to your folks." He was still chuckling when he closed the door.

Myrtle Albertina walked slowly to the next house and knocked. It wasn't a pretty house but a pretty woman answered.

"Shh," she said, smiling and putting her finger to her lips. "Baby's asleep."

"Oh," whispered Myrtle Albertina. "Would you like a picture of your baby?"

"What do you mean?"

"My uncle takes very good pictures. His name is Harvey Stevens and his photograph gallery is on Mill Street next to the livery stable."

"You don't have to whisper if you talk soft. What does your uncle charge?"

"He made a big picture of me for one dollar."

"Hmmm, how much for small?"

"Half a dollar, I think."

"All right." She folded her arms. "You can put me down."

"For when?"

"Tomorrow?"

"Oh no, it has to be after next week. Uncle Harvey won't be free till then."

"All right."

"Would June fifteenth be a good day?"

"Make it morning. Baby sleeps all afternoon."

Myrtle Albertina turned the pages, marked one June 15 and carefully wrote, "10 o'clock— Mrs. . . ." She hesitated and the pretty woman laughed. "Brock's the name," she said. "B-r-o-c-k. The baby's name is Ira. I-r-a."

"Will you remember?"

"Oh sure. I'll mark it on the calendar. Tie a string around my finger too, for good measure."

"Thank you. Good-by."

" 'Bye."

At the gate Myrtle Albertina turned back. "I forgot to tell you something. If my uncle doesn't get enough work he may have to go away. If he does, I'll let you know."

"Good luck to him, then," Mrs. Brock said.

Myrtle Albertina almost danced along to the next house and up the path to knock at the door. No one answered. No one answered at the next one either. She climbed the hill as the houses did, up and up. One house held two white-haired ladies, sisters, who made her come in, gave her cookies and listened with bright eyes to everything she said. But they couldn't afford to have their pictures taken. Not right now, anyway. Maybe next year, they said.

At another house a lady opened the door just a crack and closed it again. Another wanted to see a sample of Uncle Harvey's work. Another said she'd think about it.

Myrtle Albertina was glad Madame La Rue's house was next. Madame La Rue's eyes sparkled when they saw her but after Myrtle Albertina had explained what she was doing, they filled with black sunbeams.

"Annette. Come, *chérie*. To see Myrtle Albertina, who has fine new idea for Uncle Harvey."

"Where's Tuley?" asked Annette.

"I don't want him to know about this. Because it's a secret."

"I'll tell him." Annette's eyes danced.

"Please, Annette."

"I wouldn't tell, Myrtle Albertina. Has Major come home?"

"He wasn't there after school but maybe he is now."

"Perhaps right now," said Madame La Rue, "he sniff, sniff around and wonder to himself, why has not Myrtle Albertina come home?"

Myrtle Albertina laughed. "I wish I could be home right now and know for sure."

"*Maman,* I wish I had a dog like Major."

"Only *one* Major. Now, Myrtle Albertina, what of uncle's book? You wish me to put down day and hour for Annette's portrait to be taken. Is that so?"

"Yes. Like this." Myrtle Albertina showed her Mrs. Brock's name.

Madame La Rue took the book and slowly flipped the pages without looking at them. She seemed to be thinking. She was still thinking when the mine whistles blew for five o'clock.

"I have to go now, Madame La Rue, or Aunt Eva will ask where I've been. Besides, tonight is a very important night. We're going to see Papa and Mama after supper."

"But if you go into family with book, they will see and, poof, the secret will be gone. Leave it with me and I fill in time for Annette's picture. You come tomorrow and bring schoolbook so we can hide this one inside."

"I was going to start next door anyway tomorrow so that will be fine. Please wish me luck about Major. Good-by."

CHAPTER 11

Aunt Eva Has Callers

As Myrtle Albertina arrived at Uncle Harvey's, puffing, Tuley met her at the gate. He was waving a newspaper.

"Did Major come?"

"No. But look. This is the important thing I had to do today. To see if they'd put in the story I gave them last night. Remember? When I went out. And here it is. Read it."

"The print wiggles in the sun. You read it."

"Well, the big print says, LOST OR STRAYED, and here's the rest. Listen . . .

"Myrtle Albertina Martin has been having a double-trouble time. First, her father, Ed Martin, was caught in a cave-in at the Red Dog mine and is recovering at the hospital in Gold Town. Now, her dog, Major, has disappeared . . ."

A sudden breeze whipped the paper back in Tuley's face. "Help," he laughed, "wait a minute."

"Does it say more?"

"Yep." He shook the paper, folded it and went on:

> "Major is known to many of our townspeople as a well-behaved and popular dog. Any news as to his whereabouts will be gratefully received by Myrtle Albertina or her family."

"That's fine, Tuley. I didn't know that's where you went last night. To put a piece in the paper. I didn't even think of doing anything like that. But I think it's the best idea you could have. Because everybody reads the paper."

"Father thinks so too. He just came home."

"Is Aunt Eva here?"

"Sure. And she's excited too, about something."

As they went in Aunt Eva looked up, flushed and smiling, from the bread dough she was kneading. "Hello, Scallywags," she said. "I've just been telling Harvey my news. Mrs. Van Metre and Mrs. Wing came to have tea with me today. Only they brought the cookies because they knew I'd been busy at school. Do you know what they said, Tuley? That they'd like to have your father take Ruby Pearl's and Thelma's pictures if we plan to stay."

"What do you say, Father?"

Uncle Harvey winked at him. "It's a long time since I've seen my wife so happy and gay." He caught Aunt Eva's hand and, before she could warn him, he kissed it, smearing flour all over his face.

"Look at Father," Tuley cried, exploding into giggles while Aunt Eva laughed so hard she had to wipe her eyes on her apron.

Uncle Harvey rubbed his handkerchief over his face and wiggled his eyebrows at them.

"Doesn't my news make you feel a little gay, too, Mr. Stevens?" Aunt Eva sank her hand into the dough, kneaded it for a moment, and lifted both hands and looked at him as though she were asking him still another question. Then she threw her arms around him, flour and all.

Myrtle Albertina felt something like pink

bubbles rising in her. Did Aunt Eva mean . . . did Uncle Harvey . . . She grinned shyly at Tuley and he grinned shyly back. He turned a wild somersault and knocked a chair over on himself.

Myrtle Albertina giggled. "You'll hurt yourself and have to stay in the hospital with Papa."

"Hospital! Heavens, I'd forgotten about tonight. I'll give you all supper right away. Myrtle Albertina, I ironed your blue dress and—"

"Aren't you going with us?" Uncle Harvey asked.

"Having callers has made me too late with the bread. If I don't bake it this evening it will rise all over the place. Besides we need it for lunches tomorrow. Really, I'd like to stay home and catch my breath since I'll be seeing Mary and Ed soon."

Myrtle Albertina watched her cut the dough into two parts, pat each into shape and pop them into bread pans to rise. "Better hurry to set the table, dear," Aunt Eva said.

After that everything happened in a pleasant rush until they drove out of the livery stable and started toward Gold Town.

The buggy was a fringed-top two-seater, with

Uncle Harvey on the front seat and Myrtle Albertina and Tuley in back. The big gray horse with black mane and tail trotted so snappily that the bells on his harness rang.

Myrtle Albertina clung to the seat and breathed deep of the sweet warm air that pushed against her face. Uncle Harvey sang as he drove, a deep "Ta ra da boom de a, ta ra da

boom de a," and when he stopped, Tuley started. "Oh, I come to California with a heart both strong and bold, and have been up to the diggings . . ."

"Look at those mountains, would you!" exclaimed Uncle Harvey. "Seem almost close enough to touch."

Myrtle Albertina looked. Bowls for the stars, she thought, and remembered. "I made my own song, once," she whispered to Tuley.

"Sing it."

She giggled. "Maybe I've forgotten."

"Go ahead. Try."

"It starts, The world is deep and high and wide . . . the world is wonderful," she went on slowly. "Deep is for mines . . ."

"Go on."

"Deep is for mines, thumpety-thump . . . high is for . . . mountains, bowls for the stars . . ."

Watching Tuley's pleased face made her laugh so hard that she could hardly go on. "Do you think it's silly?" she asked.

"Of course not. Sing the rest."

"Wide for all people, hello, hello . . . this wonderful world for me."

Tuley whistled. "Say, that's pretty good. Sing it again."

After she had, he repeated the words. "Did I say it right?"

She nodded. "Now you sing it. Because you're a Cornishman and Cornishmen are the best singers."

"What's that about a Cornishman?" Uncle Harvey asked.

"Myrtle Albertina made a song, Father. Listen." He sang it. "Good, huh?"

"It certainly is. Teach it to me and we'll all sing it."

As they rode and sang, everything seemed to make music with them—the sound of the horse's hoofs, the turning wheels, the throb of the stamp mills, a train whistling at the tunnel.

They sang her song over and over but, as they clattered across the high river bridge into Gold Town, Myrtle Albertina was suddenly trembling too much to sing any more.

She was trembling because she couldn't wait to see Mama and Papa. But in the hospital, when she left Uncle Harvey to go to them, she felt too bashful to open their door. She opened it very softly and Papa saw her right away.

"Mary," he asked in a surprised voice, "am I dreaming? Or is there really a pretty little jay bird at our door?"

Mama swung on her heel, arms out, and Myrtle Albertina threw herself into them. "Oh, honey, honey." Mama's eyes were full of tears as she held her at arm's length to look at her, then hugged her again.

"All right, Chick," Papa said, sitting straight up in bed, "it's my turn now."

Myrtle Albertina grinned. "Is your leg almost well?"

"It is. Come here. What's the matter? Don't I get a kiss?"

She laughed and took two steps toward him. "That bandage makes you look like a king, Papa. With a white crown on your head."

"A king, huh?" He reached and pulled her close. "I am that. King of the Martin family anyway. What's the news from Eureka Hill?"

"Aunt Eva couldn't come because her bread was late. She had callers and was so happy. Oh, there's Tuley now, Papa. And Uncle Harvey."

Mama turned to meet them with her hands outstretched. "What's this about callers and such? Myrtle Albertina was just telling us."

158

Uncle Harvey laughed and winked at Papa.

"Any change of plans?" Mama asked.

Uncle Harvey rumpled Tuley's hair. "Oh, well, let's just say that we won't finish packing tonight."

"Stay with us, Harvey," Papa cried. "Things will get better right along. You'll see. Hello, Dr. Dunn. Come right in. You know Harvey, don't you, and Tuley? And our big, grown-up daughter?"

"Good evening, all. Mary," Dr. Dunn pretended to scold, "can't you keep this patient of ours quiet till he gets out of here?"

"In case you don't know, Doctor," Papa said, "this fellow Harvey is one man who has sense enough to stay out of the mines. We're hoping he'll be the Mother Lode's leading photographer one of these days."

Dr. Dunn grinned, reached for Uncle Harvey's hand as though he meant to shake it and showed it to Papa. "Pretty rough hand for a photographer, I'd say."

Papa looked puzzled. Mama frowned. "You haven't decided to give up your own work?"

Dr. Dunn laughed and hit Uncle Harvey on the back. "I thought it was about time some-

body let the cat out of the bag. Tell your father
what I'm talking about, Myrtle Albertina. I
have to see another patient now."

"Uncle Harvey's working for you. In the
mines. So you won't have to lose your pay."

Papa and Mama both stared at Uncle Harvey,
shaking their heads.

"But he still doesn't like it," Tuley said.

"What a fellow you are," Papa said, wringing
Uncle Harvey's hand. "How can I ever thank
you? Why I . . ."

"You don't have to worry about thanking me,
Ed. I've been all right. I've learned things."

"Golly," Papa said and took a deep breath.
"And on top of everything else, you had to have
Myrtle Albertina at your house. Were you and
Eva able to stand that?"

"Yes, we bore up fine. Matter of fact, we're
richer for it because Myrtle Albertina has
shared some of her wonderful friends with us.
We—"

"Papa, Uncle Harvey knows lots of people
now. Young Joe and Mrs. Martinez and Madame La Rue and Ah Sam and Ray Harris' father
and . . . who else, Tuley?"

Papa laughed happily. "Never mind, Son. I

160

get the idea. My daughter's been busy as usual. When's school out, anyway? Next week sometime?"

"Tomorrow," cried Tuley and Myrtle Albertina at once.

"Shhh," Mama said. "This is a hospital, remember."

They would have been reminded anyway, for a nurse came right then to tell them it was time for visitors to leave.

"When are you coming home, Mama?"

"Monday, we think."

Myrtle Albertina kissed her and Papa good night, whispered, "See you soon," and ran after Uncle Harvey and Tuley down the hall.

No one said much going home. Myrtle Albertina thought each one must be feeling as she did, too sleepy to think of anything—Major, pink bubbles, appointment books or the last day of school—just a loose bundle of sleepiness. She tried to say so to Tuley but he only grinned and pointed to the sky.

"Bowls for the stars," he sang drowsily.

"You two better climb up here with me," Uncle Harvey said. "I don't want you to go to sleep and fall off the seat."

"Oh, Father," Tuley snorted, "you think we're babies or something!"

Uncle Harvey laughed a little, sang a little and was silent. When they reached the livery stable he helped them down and told the man who took the horse that he had already paid Mr. Hartung.

The first thing they noticed as they stepped into the street was that there were no lights next door.

"Hey Father, Mom-Eva wouldn't go to bed before we got home, would she?"

Uncle Harvey didn't answer. He dashed through the gate and up the steps with Tuley after him.

Myrtle Albertina was wide awake now. She could hear Uncle Harvey calling Aunt Eva and she could smell smoke. She stumbled after the others in the dark, afraid suddenly to stay outside or to go in.

There were sounds of Aunt Eva coughing and of Uncle Harvey and Tuley slamming through the house. Shaking from head to foot, she started to feel her way along the walls to the kitchen. The smoke stung her eyes and made it hard to breathe.

"I—" Aunt Eva coughed. "Here I am, Harvey, in here. I'm all right . . . can you light the lamp?"

"I will, Mom-Eva," Tuley cried.

Myrtle Albertina heard him fumble at the matchbox by the stove and in a moment lamplight flickered into the smoke-gray room. Uncle Harvey's arms were around Aunt Eva and he was looking into her face.

"I'm all right," she said, "really I am, dear. I was . . ." When she started to cough again Uncle Harvey dipped a towel into the water pitcher and wiped it gently over her face.

"I don't know where all the smoke came from," she gasped. "I . . ."

Suddenly Uncle Harvey's face changed. "Tuley," he ordered, "take the ladder by the back porch and climb up on the roof. See if anything's wrong with the chimney. Myrtle Albertina, open the windows. All of them."

Myrtle Albertina ran through the house trying to do as he had asked. Some windows wouldn't open. When she came back to the kitchen, Uncle Harvey was fanning the rest of the smoke through the doorway with a folded newspaper and Aunt Eva sat in her rocking chair, running her hands thoughtfully through her hair.

"I'd got an overdose of smoke before I realized the house was full of it," she said. "You know how it is, things happen so quickly. But I still can't think why . . . I had a good fire going to bake the bread and the damper was right because I checked it. It was when the smoke snuffed the light out that I— Why, Tuley, what's the matter?"

"What did you find, Son?"

"This." Tuley thrust a slab of wood at his father. His black hair stood up and his whole body looked stiff with anger. "It was over the chimney. With this paper nailed to it." He held it so they could see the big printed words:

JAILBIRDS NOT WANTED
BY CITIZENS OF EUREKA HILL

Uncle Harvey's breathing shook him as he tore the paper into pieces and threw it into the stove. Watching him, watching Tuley throw the slab out the door, Myrtle Albertina felt as though the bottom had fallen out of the world. She tiptoed, trembling, to the window and stood there gripping the windowsill, not knowing

what to do. The light from the kitchen touched
the tree of heaven making each leaf look bright
and special but the joy she usually felt at such
noticing didn't come. Only a rush of wishing
came—a wish that she had Major to hug, that
such things as just happened couldn't, that she
could do something to comfort the silent people
in the room behind her, that . . .

"Harvey," asked Aunt Eva, "what are you
thinking?"

"I'm thinking we've had enough. If it's all
right with you, Eva, I'm through. We'll finish
packing this weekend and be ready to go as
soon as possible after Mary and Ed come
home."

Everything was quiet until Uncle Harvey
spoke again. "Eva . . . Tuley . . . you do understand?"

"Yes, Father, we do." Tuley's voice was still
angry, and firm, as though he would be glad
to go.

CHAPTER 12

"I Heard a Dog Barking"

IT SEEMED impossible that they could be starting off for the last day of school as though
nothing had happened. But they were.

"Listen, darlings," Aunt Eva said as she
caught up to them, "I don't think we should
speak of last night at all, do you?"

Tuley grunted. "Wouldn't give anybody that
much satisfaction."

Myrtle Albertina sighed. "Tuley, do you still
have the paper that tells about Major?"

"Sure. But it's no good. It didn't help."

"Maybe it—"

"Major's not here, is he?" Tuley asked crossly.
"If he had been, then—"

"Tuley," Aunt Eva asked him gently, "let's
try, in spite of everything, to make this a pleasant last day of school."

167

Tuley scowled. "I can still smell smoke."

"Very well. But I hope you can also smell a sweet June morning."

"With locust trees in bloom, too," Myrtle Albertina said, "and big old thunderheads piling up the sky."

"She's always noticing things like that." Tuley smiled at Aunt Eva, and Aunt Eva smiled back.

In the schoolyard, Annette ran to meet them. "I love last days of school, don't you?"

"This is my last day of school here, *ever*," Tuley said and his face looked queer as though he wished he hadn't said it.

But in a moment, Myrtle Albertina heard him say it again. "Hey, Skinny, this is my last day of school in Eureka Hill."

"It is not, I bet." Skinny turned to Myrtle Albertina and winked. "We're not going to let you go. Are we, Myrtie?"

She turned away. Skinny was always making promises he couldn't keep—promises to get gold for Uncle Harvey, to find Major, to keep Tuley from going away.

"Myrtle Albertina, did Major come home?" asked Lupita.

Myrtle Albertina shook her head. "No. But I

saw my mother and father. We rode to the hospital in a livery-stable buggy and it was fun. We sang and—" She stopped because all she could think of was what happened when they got back.

"And what?"

"And I wish and wish Major would come home."

"We used to have a dog who was always making little trips."

"Don't forget, Myrtle Albertina," Annette interrupted, "you're coming to my house this afternoon."

Myrtle Albertina shook her head.

"You have to get the appointment book. Remember?"

"It's no use, Annette. They're going away."

"But before they go—"

"They're going right away almost."

"Isn't she the gloomy one?" Annette asked Lupita, acting smarty and rolling her eyes.

Myrtle Albertina was glad when the school bell rang. But when, in class, it was her turn to tell what she was going to do during vacation, she could only shake her head and say she didn't know.

At recess when Mr. James, the school principal, stood on the school steps and clapped his hands, she didn't want to listen. She knew he was going to talk about Tuley because he always talked about the ones who were going away.

The schoolyard was quiet in a moment as everyone crowded around. "I'm sorry to tell you that one of us does not plan to return in September," Mr. James said. "Tuley, tell us what you are going to do."

"We're moving to San Francisco." Tuley stood red-faced, looking down at his shoes. "Father's going to take pictures there and I'll probably help him. San Francisco's a big city with horsecars and beaches and ships." He shrugged. "Later, if we want to, we may just travel around."

"That sounds like an interesting life."

"I guess so," Tuley said, "but I'd rather stay here. My father wants us to see some of the world, though." He started to explain as he had to Myrtle Albertina the day they played Hare and Hound in the snow. But he didn't go on. He crossed his feet, uncrossed them, tried to wiggle his eyebrows as Uncle Harvey did and grinned.

"We're very sorry you're leaving us, Tuley."

Right away Tuley's face darkened and he looked at Mr. James, so still and straight that Myrtle Albertina held her breath.

"Someone isn't sorry, Mr. James," he said. "Someone is very, *very* glad." Turning, he ran up the steps to the porch, ducked around the schoolhouse and was gone.

Myrtle Albertina was going to dash after him when someone jerked her braids, holding her back.

"What's your hurry?" Skinny asked.

"Let go my hair. I want to find Tuley."

"Shh, Myrtie, listen," Skinny whispered. "He wouldn't want a girl running after him in front of all these kids."

"He wouldn't mind *me*."

"I want to tell you something. Look under Major's blanket tomorrow."

"D'you know something about Major?"

"No. This doesn't have anything to do with him. It's something I promised. Under his blanket. On the back porch at your house, not Tuley's. Hey, there's the bell. See you later."

When she went to Aunt Eva's classroom after school, Tuley was there helping her gather her books together. "Here's your report card, Tuley. Mr. James asked me to give it to you."

"It's prob'ly no good. It never is."

"It is this time."

He smiled as he looked at it and Aunt Eva, watching, smiled too. "Tuley, if you'll take the books home for me, Myrtle Albertina and I will go right over to her house. We want to make things clean and cheery there before Ed and Mary come home."

After Tuley had left them, they walked on slowly. The air was breathlessly hot and so still that the afternoon seemed to be sleeping. Or waiting.

"Thunderstorm weather," sighed Aunt Eva as they stopped on the bridge in the shade.

Myrtle Albertina was thinking of all that had happened since she had stood here with Papa. "Aunt Eva, isn't it funny that a month can seem like a year?"

"Yes," said Aunt Eva as they walked on, "but for someone who doesn't want time to pass, a month can also seem like a week."

172

The house on the hill stopped looking lonely almost as soon as they arrived. Aunt Eva raised shades, opened windows, beat and hung pillows in the sun while Myrtle Albertina swept.

She swept the front porch and the steps. She swept the back porch, trying not to look at Major's empty blanket.

"That's a great help, pet," Aunt Eva said, coming to the door to shake a dustcloth. "Whee, just look at those dark clouds, will you? Here's Tuley already. Hello, there," she said and went inside.

Tuley puffed and pushed his damp hair back from his forehead.

"Did you see any friends?" Myrtle Albertina asked.

"No, I didn't want to." He lowered the well bucket with a splash. "I came a secret way along the creek and through Clemo's orchard." He hauled till the bucket lifted. "Want a drink?"

"Myrtle Albertina," called Aunt Eva, "someone's here to see you."

She ran through the house to the front door. "Oh, hello, Mr. Cunningham. Did you bring butter for us?"

"Not today. Figured to do that Monday so's it'll keep fresh. Figured to give your ma a special fancy pat with the acorn design on top."

"Oh."

"I stopped at your uncle's place and when I didn't find you there I thought I just might find you here. You see, I read in the paper about your dog being lost."

"Tuley. Come here. Quick."

"I always thought that Major of yours was a very fine dog. You know that?"

She felt her eyes watching Mr. Cunningham's. "First when I heard something out by Mordecai Wright's place, I didn't think a thing but—"

"Myrtle Albertina," Aunt Eva warned, "you mustn't get your hopes up."

"My hopes *are* up and Tuley's are too. Aren't they, Tuley? Mr. Cunningham, what did you hear?"

"Your aunt's right about the hopes. All I can report is a bark. That isn't much, is it? Just a bark. Heard it first the middle of the week when I came in with eggs. In the woods, about midway between my place and town, it was. Heard it again on the way home. Must say, though, I

174

didn't hear it today. Forgot about it till I read the piece in the paper. Mind you, I don't say it was your dog. Just figure it could have been."

"Would that have been about two miles from here, where you heard it?" Tuley asked.

Myrtle Albertina frowned. "Major could easily come home from there."

"It was a dog's bark, all right. Steady, going on and on, but sounding far away. Or weak. Reason I thought about it, I was surprised Mordecai Wright might have got himself a dog. Never knew him to have any pets around but wild ones. Which, I must say, he makes as tame as any."

"You think the barking was near his place?" Aunt Eva asked. "Isn't he the Negro man who sometimes helps Eureka Hill ladies with their cleaning? If so, he's much liked and respected. You don't think he'd lock Major up?"

"No, Miss Eva, I don't. I don't think Mordecai Wright would lock up any living thing. And another person's dog? No, *ma'am!*"

"Then why . . ." Myrtle Albertina twisted her braids nervously. "If it is Major, why doesn't he come home?"

"Let's find out," Tuley said, starting down the steps.

"Wait, Tuley," Aunt Eva said, "it's too late to walk that far today."

"Oh, Aunt Eva, please. We'll hurry."

"Honest we will, Mom-Eva."

"It's going to rain."

"I can drop them off on my way, Miss Eva, if you like. That way, they'd only have to walk back."

"But it's clouding over so fast."

"If it's Major, Aunt Eva, he must have waited and waited."

"We'll be all right, Mom-Eva."

"Remember, young ones," Mr. Cunningham frowned and shook his head, "I only heard a bark. Any dog barks."

Aunt Eva looked from Mr. Cunningham to Myrtle Albertina and Tuley. "I guess it shouldn't take long to find out if it is Major. So, if you'll promise to hurry right back . . . Remember, Uncle Harvey and I will be waiting. Thanks for your trouble, Mr. Cunningham."

"No trouble. Climb on," he called as he hurried after Myrtle Albertina and Tuley. "Whoa there, Lady." He reached for the reins and climbed up beside them.

Aunt Eva waved as they drove away, then swooped to hold her skirts as a gust of wind lifted them around her.

They drove down the hill, out past the courthouse, and through the cut where the narrow-gauge train was switching. They passed so close to a mine that they could hear nothing but the roar of the mill and the rumble of ore cars. They passed Big Joe and Young Joe walking toward their campoody with loads of wood on their backs, and waved to them.

"Friends of yours?" asked Mr. Cunningham.

They nodded.

"Say, young man, I hear you and your family are fixing to leave town. I hope I heard wrong."

"You heard right, Mr. Cunningham."

"That's a real shame. I, for one, like your folks very much. Land sakes, here we are already. Yes, siree. I heard the barking right along this stretch."

They rode in silence for a moment, trying to listen, as big piles of cloud boiled faster and faster in a darkening sky and the trees lashed in the wind.

"Whoa, Lady."

"I can't hear anything special," Tuley said.

"Shhh," Myrtle Albertina whispered.

"Down you get, kids. Wish I didn't have to milk, I'd go along with you."

They thanked him and clambered down. "Now you let me know if you find him." He chuckled. "Just put it in the newspaper."

They waited for the sound of Lady's hoof-beats to die away, then listened. And listened. There were many sounds in the woods but none of them was a bark.

"Let's call him," Tuley said.

Myrtle Albertina was listening too hard to answer.

"Maj . . . or! Maj . . . or!"

"Wait, Tuley, listen. Do you hear a teensy sound?"

He listened again. "Sure, but not from a dog. Do you?"

She strained to hear, then sighed and shook her head. She wondered how she could have been so excited about Mr. Cunningham's news. As if they had expected Major, missing for two days, to come bounding to meet them.

178

"I Heard a Dog Barking"

"Let's separate," Tuley suggested. "So we can search two ways at once. You take the short cut over the hill and I'll take the creek trail and meet you at Mordecai Wright's." Without waiting for an answer, he was off, calling as he went, "Maj . . . or. Major!"

Myrtle Albertina started slowly up the hill, peering behind every bush and tree for a flash of fur, starting at every moving shadow.

"Major! Maj . . . or!" The last of the sun slid under darkness and a drop of rain struck her chin.

When the wind became so noisy that she could scarcely hear anything else, she lay down and listened with her ear against the earth, as Papa had told her the Indians did. She pressed so close that pine needles scratched her face and pricked through her dress, but she didn't move. She was straining to hear a small new sound, so small she had to hold her breath to hear, or *seem* to hear, a low faint whining.

Frantically she scrambled to her feet and ran in a wide searching circle. "Major? . . . Major?" She frowned at the wind which wouldn't let her hear, lay down again to listen, and

jumped up almost at once. The sound seemed closer now. Over there, maybe. Oh surely right over there.

"Tuley," she shouted, "come quick."

She dived around a mass of manzanita bushes and stopped. The edge of an old shaft as deep as a well fell away at her feet.

"Oh!" She went down on her knees, bending forward as far as she dared. "Oh, Major boy, poor little dog. No wonder you couldn't come home."

Major whined wildly, waving his tail and shivering with gladness as he clawed at the side of the shaft and she ran around it, testing its crumbling edge for a way to get down. "Don't worry, I'll get you," she crooned, "I'll get you."

Never, never go near a shaft. Papa's words came to her as real as though he were there, and she stopped. If Tuley . . . No, it was dangerous for Tuley too. I'll find Mr. Mordecai, she thought, and raced up the hill calling Tuley all the way. When she reached the top and saw Mr. Mordecai's cabin in the distance, she called his name instead.

Lightning, zigzagging across the dark spread wings of the clouds, and the roar of thunder, answered her. Then she saw Mr. Mordecai. He was starting up the trail toward her, his lean old body bent against the wind.

"You calling Mordecai, miss?"

"Yes, Mr. Mordecai. I've found my dog—he's been lost—in a shaft over this hill. Will you help us get him out, please?"

Mr. Mordecai stopped. He rubbed his grayish hair with a big dark hand and thought. "Better go get us a rope," he said and turned back to the cabin.

As Myrtle Albertina waited she watched for Tuley. When he didn't come she decided he had heard her call and cut across the hill.

"Didn't you hear Major barking, Mr. Mordecai?" she asked as he climbed back up to her with a rope in his hand.

"I been away, except at night, for a week, helping in the town. If I heard him nighttimes, I likely thought he was a coyote." She had to run to keep up with him. "Seems like God's poor creatures aren't safe anywhere from the works of man. Many's the time I wonder why, when miners finish with the holes they make, they don't fill them in again."

"Myrtle Alber . . . tina," called Tuley's voice.

"We're coming," she cried. "Mr. Mordecai and I are coming right away."

When they reached the top of the hill, there was no sign of Tuley. Puzzled, Myrtle Albertina hesitated, looking around for him. Then she led Mr. Mordecai to the shaft, looked down and gasped. Tuley, as well as Major, was looking up at her.

"Tuley! Oh, my goodness."

Tuley blushed and grinned sheepishly. "I thought I could get him out and surprise you. But the earth didn't hold."

"Did you hurt yourself?"

"No."

"Is Major all right, do you think?"

"Yes, but he's half starved. You ought to feel his ribs. Look how he's clawed the side of the shaft here."

"Likely wore himself plumb out doing it, too." Mr. Mordecai had tied one end of the rope to a tree and now he tied the other around his waist. "You think you can lift him, boy?"

"Yes, sir." Grunting, Tuley lifted Major and held him.

Mr. Mordecai got down on the ground, stretched out and carefully, slowly wormed his way to the edge of the shaft. "We don't want to get this man down there, too," he said. "Taking it easy so the dirt's not so likely to slide."

"Just one more minute, Major," Myrtle Albertina said and at the sound of his name he almost leaped from Tuley's arms.

"Hang on to him," Mr. Mordecai warned and reached down. "Can you lift him a mite higher, boy?"

Tuley took a deep breath, braced himself and heaved Major as Mr. Mordecai reached, grasped him firmly and, wriggling back from the shaft, set him down within reach of Myrtle Albertina's arms.

"Now *I'm* coming," Tuley yelled.

"No, boy, wait. Don't try to climb out that way. You want to be buried alive? Just you wait." He pressed his hands to the earth, pulled himself slowly to his knees and stood up. He untied the rope from his waist and threw it to Tuley. "Tie it around you before you start climbing. Then if the dirt slides we can pull you up. See what—" A curtain of wind-driven rain beat over them, drowning out his voice.

"I Heard a Dog Barking"

Myrtle Albertina shivered and held Major close. She watched Tuley tie the rope, test it for holding and pull himself out of the shaft hand over hand, like a monkey.

A blaze of lightning forked through the sky and from the distance, where it struck, came the sound of a tree crashing.

"We better get us down to Mordecai's right away," the old man said. "Can you walk all right, doggy?" He felt Major's back and legs, then patted his head. "Get along, all of you, down to my place out of the storm. Hustle, now."

The inside of Mr. Mordecai's cabin was as clean and bright as Mama's kitchen. An iron pot and a teakettle steamed away on the black-polished stove. Behind it, hanging in a row on the wall, were a dishpan, a long-handled dipper and a frying pan. The pine table was scrubbed white, the bunk in the corner was neatly made. But the floor, which had been clean when they came in, was smeared now from muddy shoes and dripping clothes.

"I'm sorry we're messing your house, Mr. Mordecai," Myrtle Albertina said.

"No matter." Mr. Mordecai stuffed some

wood into the stove. "No matter at all." He opened a side door into a lean-to, took a pan from a screened wooden box hanging from a rafter and came back, closing the door behind him. "Here's what you need, dog. A nice little piece of leftover boiling meat."

He cut it into chunks, broke a piece of bread over it and mixed it with warm water. "There you are, sir," he said, setting it down for Major. "A meal fit for a king."

Myrtle Albertina laughed. "He thinks so too, Mr. Mordecai."

Major ate in great shaking gulps. Halfway through, he stopped, ears up, and looked at them almost as though he were smiling. Then he wolfed the rest of the food.

"He took care of that in a hurry," Tuley said.

Mr. Mordecai chuckled. "Now, time for us to have a little something." He lifted the top from the kettle and set it on the back of the stove.

"Thank you, but I think we'd better start home now, don't you, Myrtle Albertina? We promised Mom-Eva."

"Yes or she'll think she's lost us and Major too."

Mr. Mordecai shook his head. "Your folks

wouldn't thank Mordecai Wright to let you go out in this. Just sit a spell. It's only a summer storm and will soon pass." He pulled out a bench for them to sit on and dipped a mug of broth for each.

Major got up, stretched, and sat by Myrtle Albertina with his head on her knee. "Look," Tuley said, "he feels better already and so do I. This broth hits the spot, Mr. Mordecai."

"It's cozy here," Myrtle Albertina said. "I hope Aunt Eva knows we're safe and—" A clap of thunder shook the cabin.

"Ouch," Tuley said, "we're pretty lucky to be here."

While the wind blew, while the trees swayed and rain poured down the windows, they sipped and talked and waited. Mr. Mordecai told them of deer and fox he had fed in winter and of the birds, especially one wise old crippled raven who sometimes ate out of his hand. But his favorites, he said, were the raccoons. "Those little fellows have a mighty sweet tooth. Summer nights when the door is open, old Mother Coon comes with her babies trailing behind her, right into this room. They all lift their little black masks of faces to me, pretty as you please, begging for cake. They get it too, they surely do. Any wild things where you folks live?"

"Major chases them away from our place," Myrtle Albertina said. "That's the only bad thing about him. I guess he can't help it because that's the way dogs are."

"I live in town," Tuley said, "so we don't see much either. We're going to move though, to San Francisco."

Mr. Mordecai smiled. "You want to see wild things there, you'll have to hustle yourself out to the beach. Seals all over the rocks there, shining and flipping, pretty as a picture."

"Tuley doesn't want to live in San Francisco."

"I like living here best of anywhere I've ever lived. But . . . you see . . ." Tuley went on to tell about the wood on the chimney. When he flushed suddenly and stopped right in the middle of a sentence, Myrtle Albertina knew he had remembered they weren't supposed to talk about that.

Mr. Mordecai didn't seem to notice that Tuley didn't finish. "Listen to that," he said as a blast rattled the door. "Old wind trying to come right in."

There was so much knocking and rattling of

pine cones on the roof and wind at the door that Major was barking and Mr. Mordecai was lifting the latch before they realized that the last knock had really been one.

"Father."

Uncle Harvey helped Mr. Mordecai close the door against the wind. "Thank the Lord you're both safe. And Major too."

"Mr. Mordecai rescued him," Myrtle Albertina said.

"He rescued me too, Father. Because I was in the shaft with Major."

Uncle Harvey looked puzzled, then laughed. "I guess I'll understand everything sooner or later. But in the meantime, sir, I seem to be drowning you out." He shook his hat and water flew from it, sizzling against the stove.

"Mr. Mordecai, meet Uncle Harvey," Myrtle Albertina said.

"Have some broth, Uncle Harvey." Mr. Mordecai chuckled and handed him a steaming mug.

"At first, Father, after Mr. Cunningham left us in the woods, we didn't have much luck. But then . . ."

As Tuley talked, Myrtle Albertina thought he had never told a story so well. His eyes were dancing, his arms waving and, when he came to the part about falling into the shaft with Major, he laughed so hard he could scarcely go on. Listening, Mr. Mordecai laughed so hard that Uncle Harvey and Myrtle Albertina did the same.

"Even the sun's smiling," she cried as a bright shaft of light poured into the room. "Everything's so fine now, Uncle Harvey, if only you wouldn't go."

Uncle Harvey raised his eyebrows at her and finished his broth. "Even as I was driving here, I saw blue sky to the north. So, Mordecai Wright, sir, we'd best be moving. I've got a hired horse and buggy tied to a tree up the road and my wife will be a little anxious till she sees us. Come on, kids."

"All right," Tuley said. "Good-by, Mr. Mordecai." He opened the door and went out with Major after him.

Myrtle Albertina grasped Mr. Mordecai's hand. "I have to go now but Papa will bring me to see you soon."

Mr. Mordecai patted her hair while Uncle Harvey thanked him for his care and kindness. "I wish more people were like you," he said.

"Most is, Mr. Harvey. Most *really* is. Always a few chews overlong on wormwood. But, was I you, I wouldn't pay too much mind to such."

"What's wormwood, Uncle Harvey?"

"Bitterness," Uncle Harvey said as he and Mr. Mordecai looked at each other, steadily looked into each other's eyes.

"Mordecai Wright knows a little about such things. Quite a little, Mr. Harvey, sir."

Without a word Uncle Harvey grasped both of Mr. Mordecai's hands in his, held them for a moment, bowed and walked out.

Tuley was already climbing the trail. "Thanks for saving us and everything," he called back.

Myrtle Albertina waved to Mr. Mordecai and hurried after the others over the slippery, steaming-wet pine needles. The trees still swayed, but gently, and the air was wood-sweet and cool.

"Look, Father. Come over here. This is the shaft where it happened. Careful of the edge there, Myrtle Albertina."

She had to smile. "You're the one to be careful, Tuley Stevens. You and Major."

Uncle Harvey, an arm around each of them, looked down and heaved a great sigh. "I'm *very* thankful for Mordecai Wright," he

said. As he turned away he bent for a moment
over a pile of dumped rock and winked at Myrtle Albertina. "No nuggets today, Miss Martin?"

She smiled and shook her head. Her nugget-
searching time seemed long ago. Now, as she
walked with Uncle Harvey, she could only think
of what Mr. Mordecai had said.

"Uncle Harvey, do you think Mr. Mordecai's
right? About not paying attention to—"

"Sure, he's right. Right as rain. But it's easier
said than done, except by a truly good man.
That's what Mordecai Wright is. He's also, most
likely, a very brave one. I'm afraid I can't say
as much for your Uncle Harvey."

Myrtle Albertina kept her eyes on his face,
waiting for him to say more, but he only smiled,
patted her cheek and hurried ahead of her down
the trail.

CHAPTER 13

Kit Carson Climbs a Tree

MYRTLE ALBERTINA opened her eyes, stretched, and yawned deeply. Then, remembering, she felt down beside her bed.

"Major," she whispered and at once she felt the breeze from his waving tail. "Here," she invited and he stood with his front paws on the edge of her bed, ears up, tongue out, watching her and waiting.

She laughed and hugged him. "I'm glad-glad you're home and I bet you're glad too." She jumped out of bed, running and romping with him. She pretended to spring at him and he pranced and growled. She ducked away from him around the ferns and stumbled into two new packing boxes against the wall. Two others, which had stood half empty for so long, were full, ready for the covers to be nailed on.

She stood looking at them, thinking. "Packing, packing, packing," she muttered. "You know what that means, Major? Well, it means things a dog can't understand. It also means Tuley won't be able to play today." Angrily she pulled on her long black stockings. Then she finished dressing, leaned out and sniffed. "Major, you know what I can smell? Lots of things . . . roses . . . and horses . . . and hay . . ."

"Roses, horses and hay," she hummed, "and Tuley's going away."

Things were all going to be changed again. Monday she would be back in her own home with Mama and Papa, and maybe everything would be the way it was before, before she had known Tuley. As soon as she thought it she knew it couldn't be true. Before you had something, like for instance a friend, you couldn't miss him if he went away. But after he had his own special place in your feelings . . . She turned from the window and made a face at the packing boxes.

This strange mixed-up mood of gladness about Mama and Papa and Major, and crossness about Tuley's going away, lasted all day. It made her a smiling help to Aunt Eva one minute and a sulky one the next. Sometimes it made her giggle as she teased Tuley for worrying about her and lions while *he* went close to shafts. Other times it made her feel tears so close that she had to hide her face.

It was a hot day too, just as hot as though it had never stormed. But at the end of it, when Uncle Harvey came home, almost everything was done.

"My goodness," he exclaimed, "hasn't anyone left anything for me to do?"

"I should hope not very much," Aunt Eva said, "after you've mined all day."

"I saw Dr. Dunn on my way home. He says Mary and Ed will be in on the narrow-gauge Monday afternoon."

"What time is it due?"

"Around three. I'll check for sure at the station when I go to make arrangements for our own tickets and boxes tomorrow evening."

"We get to ride on the broad-gauge to San Francisco, don't we, Father?"

Uncle Harvey nodded. "The narrow-gauge goes to Colfax. We change to the big one there."

"Maybe you can ride it too, Myrtle Albertina. When you come to visit us."

Myrtle Albertina frowned and rubbed Major's fur the wrong way. She felt cross and sulky again.

"Whew," Uncle Harvey said after supper, "why do we have to have a fire in the stove now? It's hot enough without that."

"I'm heating water for baths," Aunt Eva said. "So each of us can have a good restful soak before bedtime. You want to be first, Myrtle Albertina?"

Uncle Harvey set the wooden washtub on the floor of the studio and Aunt Eva poured in hot, then cold water and tested it. Myrtle Albertina tested it too. "A little more cold, please," she said.

As soon as she was alone, she took off her clothes, tried one foot in the water and, taking a bar of soap, curled down in the tub. While the water was very hot, she wiggled and wiggled as she turned pinker and pinker. After it cooled, she settled down to splashing dreamily, trying to make waves big enough to break over her knees.

All the time she was soaking, soaping, washing and drying, she was thinking. Her mixed feelings weren't really mixed *up*, she decided.

It was only that a person had to be glad about some things and sorry about others, and when both happened at the same time . . . well, you just had to feel them both at once, that was all. That's just the way I've been, she thought and right away her sulkiness went.

Tuley noticed, the first thing next morning, that it was gone. "What did you do with that mean old face you were wearing yesterday?" he asked.

She giggled. "I washed it off when I bathed. And drowned it in the washtub."

"Golly, you didn't even seem like you."

"Well, she was a great help no matter how she looked, Mr. Stevens, Junior," Aunt Eva said. "By the way, when your father goes to the station, I'd like to have you and Myrtle Albertina go up to her place to water the rose bush and sprinkle the front yard. Freshen things up a little."

"All right, Mom-Eva."

They went that evening as soon as it was cool. As they walked along Mill and Main streets their footsteps made pleasant echoing sounds on the board walks. At the corner of Main and Creek Road they met the water wagon behind its span of big white horses and smelled the good earthy smell that rose as the heavy spray fell over the dusty street.

At the bridge Uncle Harvey turned toward the depot and Tuley and Myrtle Albertina went on, slowly climbing the hill. Major, seeming to be filled with joy at going home, ran. But he stopped to sniff at everything—trees, gate, front steps and back—and they caught up with him.

Tuley laughed when Major tore up the steps and went right to his blanket. "He wants to be sure things are just the way he left them."

Just at that moment, and not until then, Myrtle Albertina remembered Skinny's promise. *Look under Major's blanket.* She looked at it but it looked as it always had, with no sign of anything under it. Skinny was only fooling again, she thought.

This time Skinny wasn't. As soon as Tuley, lugging a pail of water, disappeared around the corner of the house, she looked. Something *was* there—a very small soiled box and a note.

The note was scrawled in Skinny's worst writing. "Here it is," it said. "If Tuley's pop needs it to stay, give it to him, but if he'll stay anyway, I want it back. Skinny."

Frowning, she opened the box and gulped. There, lying on a piece of pink cotton, was a beautiful nugget. It was as big as a bean and, even with the sun gone, it glowed like a buttercup.

Wondering, she turned it carefully in her fingers. Where could Skinny have found such a nugget, worth so much money but no good now to Uncle Harvey. I'll have to be very careful of it, she thought, till I can give it back.

"Hey, Myrtle Albertina, aren't you going to help?"

She tucked the nugget into its box and stuffed it quickly into her pocket. "Right now, Tuley. I'm coming."

They watered until it was almost dark, then wandered slowly back down the hill. The last yellow light was slipping away at the edge of the world and a little bright moon hung in the blue-lavender sky.

"Tuley, I'm thinking the moon's a silver comma. What are you thinking?"

"It's a pirate's knife. Sharp as anything and cold."

"You make me shiver." She giggled. "Now, what are you looking at?"

Tuley was squinting into the twilight. "Do you see somebody standing by Clemo's fence?"

"I *think* I do. Why?"

"I thought I heard—"

"That you, Tuley?" called a voice.

"That's Father." Tuley started to run.

"But Tuley, I can see now. That person is

200

Mrs. Andrews." She panted to keep up with him.

Mrs. Andrews turned to meet them. "Mr. Stevens is in the tree." Her voice was shaky and shrill. "Kit and I were strolling and happened to pass the water wagon just as the train whistled by us. Well, that frightened the horses so they reared, swung the wagon sideways and threw water all over Kit and me. Kit sprang from my arms and, before I could stop him, he bolted up this tree. His leash got caught, jerked him loose and he was hanging when . . ."

She stopped for breath and Uncle Harvey's voice came calmly from the leafy darkness above their heads. "Tuley, I'm holding the cat so he won't choke. But I can't seem to hold and untangle him at the same time. Come help me. Myrtle Albertina, you keep Major quiet. Kit's not in the mood for people *or* dogs. Can you see?" he added as Tuley shinnied up the tree. "His leash is caught between those two branches by your hand, on a broken twig. Got it? All right then, here's the cat."

Kit gave a long angry yowl as Tuley dropped with him from the tree. "Here you are, Mrs. Andrews. Better be careful, he's a little riled."

Mrs. Andrews took him tenderly and tried to kiss him while Myrtle Albertina held Major and talked to him to keep him quiet.

"Getting down all right, Father? Put one foot on this knob here. Give me your hand."

Uncle Harvey jumped and landed beside them. "Whew," he said, "we made it."

Mrs. Andrews looked closely at him in the dusk. "Is that blood on your face, Mr. Stevens? Did he . . . ? Oh, Mr. Carson, you *are* the naughty one. Clawing the man who was saving your life."

Uncle Harvey laughed heartily. "Maybe he didn't want to be rescued by a black-hearted highgrader. Don't worry, Mrs. Andrews, the scratch is nothing. I'm glad I happened along and could be of help. Good evening, ma'am. And the same to you, Kit."

Uncle Harvey bowed and turned with Myrtle Albertina and Tuley toward town, still chuckling.

"Myrtle Albertina."

Myrtle Albertina looked back. "Yes, Mrs. Andrews."

"I'm sure Kit will be better behaved when he has his picture taken. Good night, *all.*"

"Good night." Myrtle Albertina almost bumped into Uncle Harvey, who had stopped, stock-still.

"What does Mrs. Andrews mean, Father?"

Uncle Harvey went on, shaking his head. "Maybe she knows what she's talking about," he told them, "but I don't."

CHAPTER 14

Myrtle Albertina's Song

MYRTLE ALBERTINA kneeled at her window and looked out at the plum tree, at the greenness of its neat new plums glowing in the soft light of evening. All the white petals it had held in May seemed as lost now as small white stars are when they fall.

The sound of Mama's and Papa's voices coming to her from downstairs made her feel homey and safe and full of love. But not joy. Because of tomorrow and Tuley's going, joy wouldn't come. It would have helped, she knew, to talk things over with Mama and Papa, but so far they had spoken only of pleasant things—how good it was to be home, how beautiful the roses looked, how kind people had been, how delicious the well water was.

"The best well water in the whole county,"

Papa had exclaimed, "best water, best daughter, best friends, best dog . . ."

Mama had laughed and told him, for goodness' sake, to stop bragging. Then Myrtle Albertina had asked them to listen to Tuley tell the story of how they almost had no dog at all.

Tuley had told it as well as he had at Mr. Mordecai's and everybody had laughed almost as hard as she and Uncle Harvey and Mr. Mordecai had then.

Once, when there was a pause in the talk, she had looked at Aunt Eva, wondering when something was to be said about going away. Aunt Eva had given her head the tiniest shake and later she had whispered that it was best to have a happy afternoon. "Time enough for the other this evening," she had said.

Myrtle Albertina turned from the window and went downstairs, feeling quivery because already it *was* this evening. She stood on the last of the stairs, noticing that the parlor door was wide open to the smells of summer, noticing that Mama was trying to make Papa rest on the sofa and Papa was refusing.

"This is home, Mary, not a hospital." He sat up straighter in his chair with both hands on his cane. "Here's our Chicken. Looking pretty solemn though, it seems to me, for a young lady who's just got her parents back."

"That's right, Pet, you do. Anything wrong?"

She couldn't think what to say. She looked from Mama to Papa and they looked at her. "Guess," she said at last.

Mama's look flashed from her out the doorway. "Here comes our other family," she said, and looked again at Myrtle Albertina. "Don't you want to tell me what's on your mind, honey, before we welcome them? We can go out in the other room for a moment."

Myrtle Albertina shook her head and Mama, watching her closely, frowned.

"Come in, all," Papa called. "Come in and make yourselves at home. Close the door, will you, Tuley." He thrust out a hand to Uncle Harvey. "I've been thinking. It's going to take a lifetime to thank you for what you've done for us."

Uncle Harvey took Papa's hand. "We can skip that, Ed. We liked what we did for you and Mary. I wish we could like what we're doing next."

"It's why I was solemn, Mama."

"We'd about decided to stay, Mary," Aunt Eva said, "but . . ."

"We're all packed," Tuley said. "We're going tomorrow."

The room was full of silence.

"I don't understand," Mama said after a moment.

Papa stood up, bracing himself on his cane. Mama motioned for him to sit down but he shook his head. "I don't either," he said. "When you visited us the other night at the hospital, we thought . . . What are you trying to do, Harvey? Take on another world before you've got this one licked?"

"This one's licked me, Ed."

"Nonsense," Mama cried, "that's—"

Before she could go on, Major sprang up, barking wildly, and the sound of voices and hurrying footsteps rushed at them as the door was thrown open.

There stood a crowd of laughing, dish-carrying people. "Surprise," they shouted and surged in—Madame La Rue and Annette, Dr. Dunn and his family, the Van Metres and theirs, Mr. and Mrs. Cunningham, Mrs. Martinez and Lupita, Mrs. Andrews without Kit Carson, Skinny

Hooper, his big brother, father and mother, Ray Harris and his father, Thelma Wing, the sheriff —so many people that Myrtle Albertina lost count.

"For he's a jolly good fellow," they sang, "for he's a jolly good fellow . . ."

"Grab hands," Skinny yelled. "Give me yours, Myrtie, and you take Tuley's."

She reached toward Tuley, who was looking as though he didn't know *what* to do.

"Oh come on, Tuley," Skinny ordered. "Take Myrtle Albertina's hand and get in the ring."

Tuley did and Annette took his other hand. Ray took hers and Thelma's, Thelma took Lupita's. Lupita took Ruby Pearl's and Ruby Pearl took Skinny's to make a big circle around Papa and Uncle Harvey.

"For he's a jolly good fellow, as nobody can deny," they sang with Skinny and Annette leading, pulling the circle close and bowing to Uncle Harvey.

Uncle Harvey was acting strange, almost like someone walking in his sleep. "What is this . . . all about . . . I . . ."

"I tell you." Madame La Rue laughed and clapped her hands to attract attention. "In one moment, after I find if all food has come safely. Has it? Good. So, Mr. Stevens, this is surprise. *Two* surprise. Number one, party. Party for Aunt, Uncle, Cousin. Is that not so, Myrtle Albertina?"

"Yes, but—" Myrtle Albertina flushed and turned to Mama. "Mama, I *did* tell her we couldn't have the party. Don't you remember, Madame La Rue, after Papa was hurt, I . . ."

"*Certainement.* You did indeed." She stood as straight and tall as her smallness would allow and spoke out in a loud, clear voice. "But we *wanted* party. For Papa, because he is well again. But most we want party for him who work in mine for Papa while he get well in hospital. For Uncle Harvey."

Uncle Harvey frowned and looked very bash-

ful. "I didn't do anything so special," he said. "Anything that anybody wouldn't have done for a friend."

"We think very special." Madame La Rue gave her head a quick nod and clapped her hands again. "Annette, bring number two surprise."

As Annette pushed something into Uncle Harvey's hands, Myrtle Albertina saw at once that it was the old appointment book that she had left with Madame La Rue.

"Myrtle Albertina start to fill it for Uncle Harvey. Then we go on doing so. You find inside many picture-taking appointments, Mr. Stevens, twenty in all—many kinds from small Kit Carson to big wedding. And more promised."

Uncle Harvey looked at his book as though it were something very precious he had lost and found again. "Thank you," he said. "This is a wonderfully kind thing you have done. But," he hesitated and his face became very serious, "I regret now, my friends, that I have no choice but to tell you the truth. We were smoked out of our house the other night and I've pledged myself never to let my wife or son go through such ugliness again. I think any man among you here would have pledged the same."

He stopped and the silence seemed to quiver, first with surprise, then with anger. Papa's eyes blazed and the scar on his forehead was bright red.

"Now that you understand why we must go away," Uncle Harvey said, "let us fully enjoy this beautiful party you have made."

"Mr. Stevens. Hey, Mr. Stevens. Listen." Skinny was tugging at Uncle Harvey's arm. "If that block of wood on your chimney is all you're bothered about . . . well, heavens to Betsy, you can stop right now. I did that myself. Because of Myrtie's idea."

Myrtle Albertina felt as though she had been knocked sideways. The shocked eyes in the still, shocked faces, the walls, the floor—everything seemed to rock as her anger grew big, big and bigger.

"Don't you dare say such a thing, Skinny Hooper. I could never have such a terrible idea."

"Myrtie, listen here." Skinny was grinning. "Whose idea was it to get nuggets to keep Tuley from going away?"

"*That* was mine, but—"

"Well, I did that to the chimney to get a nugget, see? Someone gave it to me for doing it."

There was a gasp from the crowd then a buzz of stern voices before the sheriff stepped forward and motioned for silence. "Skinny, didn't you know you were doing wrong? Very wrong?"

"Yes, sir. I guess I did. But I thought the nugget would make up for it. I thought they'd just open the doors and let the smoke out and that'd be the end of it."

"If I'd been home you wouldn't have dared," raged Tuley.

"Golly, Tuley," Skinny faltered. "I thought you were home. I only did it so you wouldn't go away."

The sheriff laid his hand on Skinny's shoulder. "Who suggested you do it, son?"

Skinny's face turned so pale that his freckles stuck out. He hung his head and moved one foot backward and forward over the brown design of the carpet.

"Tell us, Skinny," ordered the sheriff.

"I can't," said Skinny and turned to his mother, whose eyes were full of tears. "Ma, I promised I wouldn't."

Mrs. Andrews' voice interrupted, sharp and scolding. "Go ahead and tell."

Skinny shook his head.

"If you don't, I will."

He ran his foot once more over the pattern on the carpet and spoke so low that no one could hear him.

"Speak up, Skinny," Mrs. Andrews said.

"All right, then. I did it for you. So you would give me the nugget."

"He's right," Mrs. Andrews said, bobbing her head. "But now I'm sorry so you don't all have to act so hot and bothered. I made the arrangements with Skinny before I got to know Mr. Stevens. Through Kit Carson, that was." She smiled a little at the memory, then blushed as she looked around at the people in the room. No one was smiling at *her*. She tossed her head. "I told you I'm sorry. Very sorry. I was even sorry before I met Mr. Stevens. In fact, I'd made an appointment to have Kit's picture taken. So what else do you want me to do?" She threw the words at them. "Oh, I know you tried to tell me he wasn't a highgrader, that he was a good man. But I'm set in my ways and my thinking. And, what's more, I've good reason to be. Besides, it was months ago that I made that sign and offered Skinny money to use it. He got good and mad at me. But a couple of weeks ago he said he might do it for a big nugget if I had one. By that time Myrtle Albertina had told me some things about her uncle that started me thinking, but I'm not one to think that children know everything." She caught her breath and looked around with pursed mouth and darting eyes. "Well, it's plain to see how the wind blows. I know when I'm not wanted."

She started for the door but Papa stood in her way. "Wait, Mrs. Andrews, please. There's plenty of room for all of us in this town to live in peace together. So let's begin, right now."

"Get out of my way, Ed Martin. I . . . you . . . all of you . . ." For a moment her bitter busy words went on but as she swung once more to face them, Uncle Harvey went to her and held out his hand.

"I . . ." She stopped her head-bobbing and her mouth quivered. "Mr. Stevens, if you can forgive a hard-bitten old—"

Myrtle Albertina couldn't hear what she said

after that for the room had come joyously alive. Major started to bark and prance in circles and she felt like doing the same.

"Uncle Harvey, everything's going to be all right now, isn't it?"

Uncle Harvey, with one arm around Aunt Eva, beckoned to Myrtle Albertina.

"From the very first," cried Mama with her eyes shining, "Myrtle Albertina's said she'd never let Tuley go."

"Too bad," teased Uncle Harvey, "that we're all packed and ready."

"I'll unpack for you, Father," Tuley shouted.

"We'll all help," shouted the crowd.

Uncle Harvey bowed and held out his hands. "My family, friends . . . each of you . . . how can I tell you how I feel?" He rubbed his head as though trying to think. Suddenly he cried, "Ah," and snapped his fingers. "I have it, the very thing."

As everyone, smiling, watched, he pulled Myrtle Albertina and Tuley, each to one side of him, and announced, "We'll *sing* the way we feel. With Myrtle Albertina's song."

And they did.

Myrtle Albertina's Song

"The world is deep and high and wide,
   The world is wonderful;
   Deep is for mines,
   Thumpety-thump;
   High is for mountains,
   Bowls for the stars;
   Wide for all people,
   Hello! Hello!
   This wonderful world for me."